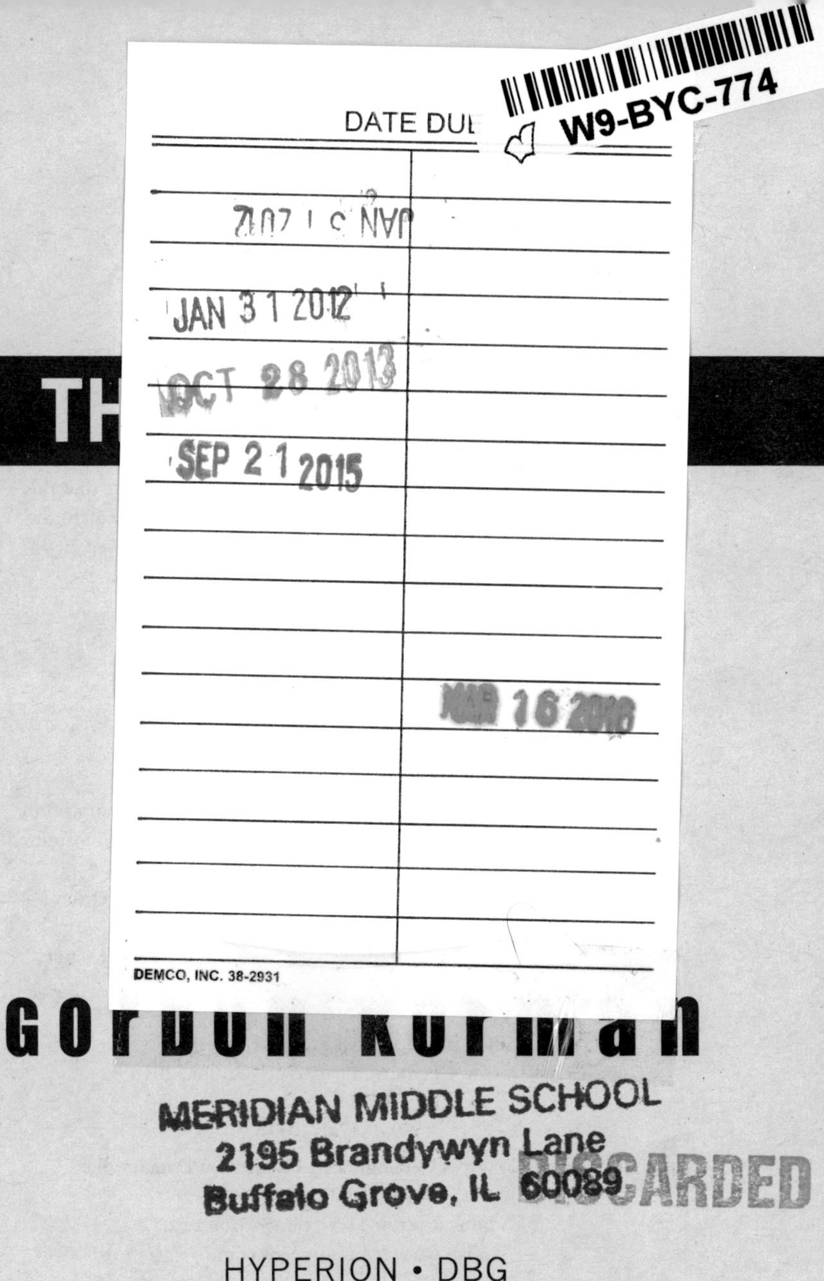

Gordon Korman

HYPERION • DBG
New York

For information address Disney • Hyperion Books, 114 Fifth Avenue, New York, New York 10011-5690.

Printed in the United States of America
First Disney • Hyperion paperback edition, 2010
10 9 8 7 6 5 4 3 2
J689-1817-1-10176
Library of Congress Cataloging-in-Publication Data on file.
ISBN 978-1-4231-0162-8
This book is set in 11.5-point Janson text.
Visit www.hyperionteens.com

For Grandma Lil, Grams, and Sy,
who put the "great" in great grandparents

Also by Gordon Korman

Schooled

Born to Rock

Son of the Mob

Son of the Mob: Hollywood Hustle

No More Dead Dogs

Jake, Reinvented

Maxx Comedy: The Funniest Kid in America

The 6th Grade Nickname Game

CHAPTER ONE

Gecko Fosse is behind the wheel of a powder blue Infiniti M45 sedan, enjoying the thrum of the idling engine and not thinking. Gecko has elevated not thinking to the level of high art. He's almost as good at it as he is at driving, and that's *very* good.

Right now he's not thinking about the fact that he's too young to hold a license—that he's still got two years to go before he even qualifies for a learner's permit. He's not thinking about what his brother, Reuben, meant when he said he needed to "pick something up" at an electronic games store that closed two hours ago.

Mostly, he's not thinking about the bald guy in the rearview mirror, sprinting up behind him, waving his arms and yelling.

"*Hey, that's my car!*"

The bald guy grabs for the door handle, but Gecko is already squealing away from the curb, grooving on the burst of acceleration. It's his favorite feeling—that boost of pure power, like a titanic hand propelling him forward.

There's the store, coming up on the left. A flick of Gecko's wrist, a tap on the brake, and the Infiniti is right there. The place is dark. No sign of Reuben and his buddies. Gecko rabbit-punches the leather of the steering wheel, producing a staccato honk of the horn. Rueben leans into the window display of Wiis, waving him urgently away. Gecko stomps on the gas and wheels around the corner out of sight.

Reuben—there's someone not to think about. This is supposed to be his new ride. Gecko's gaze darts to the ignition, which has been ripped out, a pair of wires protruding from the column. No key. Reuben and his friends think they're so gangster, but they're really more like the Keystone Cops. Leave it to them to steal a car and then wave it right in front of the guy who used to own it. And if they're dumb enough to pull something like that, who knows what they're up to inside the House of Games?

He turns left and left again, circling back onto Jackson. It's effortless. The wheel is an extension of his hands, just the way he likes it. Gecko's the car, and the car is Gecko. Not bad, this M45 . . .

Uh-oh. The bald guy's dead ahead, and he's managed to flag down a traffic cop. The cop steps right into the Infiniti's path, holding his hand out like, well, a cop. Gecko slaloms around him and then floors it. In the blink of an eye, the Infiniti is halfway down the next block. Gecko grins into the mirror. The officer and the car owner scramble helplessly in his wake.

The smile disappears abruptly as his rear view changes. The door of the shop bursts open, and out stumble Reuben and his two cronies, weighed down with huge armloads of video games. One of them actually runs into the traffic cop, bowling him over in a spray of falling boxes.

Gecko shifts into reverse. Now the acceleration is pressing on his chest, propelling him backward. Uh-oh. The light changes. A solid line of traffic is coming at him from the other direction. He presses on the gas, steering with one hand as he peers over his shoulder at the tons of metal hurtling toward him. The gap disappears in a heartbeat, split seconds to impact—

At the last instant, a tiny space opens up between the SUV and a van. Gecko swerves for it, threading the needle. The passenger mirror shatters as the van passes too close.

Gecko slams on the brakes, and Reuben and company pile in, raining disks all over the backseat. The Infiniti screams away.

His brother is the picture of outrage. "What are you doing, Gecko? You trying to get us busted?"

Gecko doesn't respond. His not thinking kicks back in. He's not thinking about the stolen car or what his brother has gotten him into *again*. From the first time Reuben saw him piloting a go-kart, Gecko's fate was sealed. A getaway-driver-in-training since age nine.

The passengers are taking inventory of the haul, squabbling over who gets what, when they first hear the sirens.

Reuben slaps his brother on the back of the head. "Get us out of here, man!"

Gecko is already up to eighty on the avenue, weaving skillfully in and around traffic, using the sidewalk when necessary. Without telegraphing his move, he squeals into an underground parking garage, dutifully taking the ticket from the machine. He sails through the tight rows of parked cars as if taking a Sunday drive on the widest boulevard in town. The exit beckons dead ahead, leading onto a different avenue, this one southbound.

The Infiniti blasts through the wooden barrier, splintering it and sending the pieces flying. In an impressive burst of horsepower, the car streaks through four lanes of moving traffic and whips around the next corner.

That's where it happens. An elderly nanny, pushing a baby carriage in front of her, steps off the curb to cross with the light. It's a split-second decision, and Gecko makes it. He wrenches the steering wheel, and the speeding car brushes the back of the shocked nanny's coat. The right front tire jumps the curb and plows up onto an old mattress leaning on a pile of trash. With the passenger side climbing and the driver's side still on the road, the Infiniti flips over. For a heart-stopping moment they are airborne, hot video games bouncing around like Ping-Pong balls.

Gravity reverses. A teeth-jarring crash.

Everything goes dark.

CHAPTER TWO

Gecko opens the dryer door and staggers back from a blast of arid heat that sears his skin and bakes the moisture out of his eyes, nose, and mouth. He reaches in, burning his fingers on the metal snaps of at least thirty orange jumpsuits.

The industrial-size equipment in the laundry room of the Jerome Atchison Juvenile Detention Center must be powered by volcanic heat, accessed straight from the earth's core, Gecko reflects, trying to blink some tears back to his eyes.

Strange that it would be hard to cry in a place like this. It took all his strength to hold himself back from bawling on day one, when they marched him through the tall gates topped with razor wire. Only thoughts of Reuben in adult prison kept him from completely going to pieces.

Atchison's probably a picnic by comparison. . . .

On the other hand, that's Reuben's problem. This

whole mess is one hundred percent his fault. Gecko was the most surprised guy in the world to wake up in the inverted Infiniti and find himself in deep trouble. Grand theft auto; accessory to robbery; driving without a license. There weren't this many charges against Al Capone.

Their mother was so shattered by Reuben's fate, she barely even noticed her younger son sinking into similar quicksand. As for his court-appointed lawyer—at the hearing, the guy seemed relieved that Gecko would be off the streets for a while.

Probably drives an Infiniti. . . .

Eventually, the jumpsuits are cool enough to be handled. Gecko teeters under the weight of an enormous armload, drops it on a table, and begins the process of folding. In thirty seconds, the sweat dripping from his brow is dotting the orange cotton. The laundry is actually considered one of the better jobs at Atchison. The road gangs come back with nasty blisters and worse attitudes, and the kitchen crews lose their appetites for months.

The attack is so sudden, so unexpected, that he's captured and immobilized before he has time to utter a sound. A pillowcase is pulled down over his head and past his shoulders to imprison his arms.

He knows exactly what's coming, and it terrifies him. This hazing ritual is legend at Atchison. He's been waiting for it—dreading it—for two months.

He tries to shrug out of the hood, but strong,

rough hands clamp around him. A voice snarls, "Don't even think it, punk!" He's aware of at least four or five people around him.

The first blow catches him on the side of the head, just above the ear. It feels like the impact of a Tomahawk missile, although he knows it's just a bar of soap being swung inside a sock. "Classes" at Atchison are a joke. No one—teacher or student—expects any learning to take place. But the inmates here could write a set of encyclopedias on how to inflict pain.

The second shot is to his rib cage. It's astounding that a mere bar of soap can hurt this much. It starts his heart racing, but no faster than his mind. His panicked thoughts are of a boy he never met—street name: Q-Bone—who was beaten so badly this way that he died of a heart attack at age fifteen. Or so the story goes.

Another explosion of pain, and Q-Bone's fate isn't hard to believe. Will Gecko Fosse be the next rumor?

All at once, the hands imprisoning him melt away, the beating stops, and there are scurrying footsteps.

"Fosse?"

Gecko struggles out of the pillowcase. Mr. Bell, the so-called school's so-called principal, is standing in the doorway of the laundry room. He's also the so-called guidance counselor. But from the sidearm he wears, everybody can tell he's just like all the other adults in this place—a jail guard.

"What are you fooling around for, Fosse? Don't you know I have to write you up for this?" At Atchison, attempted murder is the victim's fault.

It never occurs to Gecko to try to explain the situation. These people are in a business where the customer is always wrong. Besides, ratting—even on nameless, faceless kids you can't identify—earns you more than a bar of soap in here.

"Sorry," Gecko mumbles finally.

Bell sighs in exasperation. "Follow me. There's someone to see you in the office."

All through the labyrinth of corridors, Gecko racks his brain. Who came to see him? And why not during regular visiting hours, in the usual meeting area? Mom? No, not with her working two jobs, and home a hundred fifty miles away. Reuben? He's behind bars of his own, guarded by men with even bigger guns.

They pause at the security gate and wait for the attendant to buzz them through. He does and pats Gecko down for sharp objects.

"He's clean."

The office door is open, and Gecko cranes his neck eagerly to peer inside. His visitor is—he frowns. A total stranger.

The fear races back. *It's all a mistake. They've called the wrong kid. I'm going straight back to the laundry, where those guys can finish the job! I have to figure out a way to defend myself. . . .*

The stranger stands up. "Graham Fosse?"

"That's Gecko."

"All right, Gecko. Come on in. Have a seat."

Warily, Gecko sidles into the room and perches on the edge of a chair.

The newcomer turns to Bell. "Thanks. I can take it from here."

Bell is reluctant. "I don't think that's such a good idea."

"Don't worry. I can handle myself."

Bell doesn't budge. "He's outside lockup. Regulations say he has to be accompanied."

Gecko sizes up his visitor. He's about five foot nine—not tall, but not short either, and neither thin nor fat. His hair is kind of sandy—not blond, not dark; red, maybe. He doesn't have a single distinguishing feature, like a scar, birthmark, or mustache. Even his eyes are not quite blue, not quite brown, not quite green. Gecko can't imagine anything more difficult than being asked to describe him. He's practically an *un*-guy.

"I'm Douglas Healy."

Gecko waits for more. It doesn't come.

Should I know this person?

"I'm the one behind this new program you've been hearing about—the alternative living situation." Healy frowns. "Well, surely you've been told you're a candidate for . . ." His voice trails off. "No?"

Gecko doesn't know how to respond. He doesn't

want to get himself into any more trouble, but he's never heard of Douglas Healy, and has no idea what the newcomer is trying to say.

Healy's nondescript eyes flash with anger as he wheels on Bell. "It's taken more than a year to get this program approved! To get the funding in place! I've been talking to *parents*, for God's sake! Are you telling me that nobody even bothered to mention to Gecko that he's being considered?"

Bell shrugs. "This is the first I'm hearing of it. You want to see if the superintendent's in? He'd be the one to ask."

The newcomer lets out an exasperated breath. "The last thing I need is more red tape, thank you very much." He addresses the teenager in the orange jumpsuit. "Gecko, how'd you like to get out of this place? I mean right now—today."

Gecko is wary. When something sounds too good to be true, it usually is. "With you?"

"I've received a New Directions grant from the Garfield Foundation to create a living situation for boys in the juvenile detention system. A halfway house, if you will."

"Halfway to where?" Gecko asks suspiciously.

Healy smiles. "Here's how it works: you live with me and two other boys in an apartment. You go to school; you go into counseling; you do community service. To be blunt, you work your butt off and keep your nose clean. If you're looking for a vacation, this isn't it. But it also isn't juvie. 'Halfway' means halfway home. You do your time with me, and you walk away from all this. Mess up, and you're right back here."

Outwardly, Gecko betrays little emotion. Inside, though, his brain is processing feverishly. Could this be real—a chance to get out of Atchison? To erase the nightmare of the last two months? To escape the torture that awaits him in the laundry room, if not today, then soon enough?

A dozen possible problems appear in his mind. "What about my family—my mom?" he corrects himself. It's unlikely that Reuben will be a factor in anything for the foreseeable future.

Mr. Bell supplies the answer to that one. "When you're in the system, the Juvenile Justice Department is your family. We can transfer you at our discretion. From our perspective, a halfway house is just an extension of our facilities."

Gecko tries hard to keep his voice steady and his expression unreadable. "What if my mother comes to visit me and I'm not here?"

"I spoke to your mother," Healy says quietly. "She understands that you're being given a once-in-a-lifetime opportunity. You won't be seeing her anytime soon. No contact at all for the first six months. That's a condition of the grant. No phone calls, no e-mails, no letters."

"And if I say no?"

"You won't," Healy replies confidently. "Living in

jail or living free. It's not much of a decision."

Gecko nods. He made the decision back at *right now—today*. To avoid a return visit to that laundry room, he'll happily follow this unperson to the end of the earth.

CHAPTER THREE

As dreary and depressing as Atchison is, Douglas Healy's next stop makes it seem like a theme park. The Remsenville Correctional Facility is a medium-security adult prison with high walls, guard towers with fixed machine guns, and trained attack dogs at the gates.

"What's a fifteen-year-old doing in a place like this?" Healy mutters as armed sentries search the car, even checking the undercarriage with mirrors.

Gecko labors to conceal his terror behind a tight-lipped stoic expression.

Healy sees through it. "Take it easy. I'm not bringing you here. You're not even coming inside with me. There's a kid I have to see so I can make him the same offer I made you. I can only imagine what he's been through after fourteen months in a charm school like this."

Gecko stays with the gate crew while Healy

proceeds through the series of checkpoints, metal detectors, and pat-downs that will admit him to Remsenville.

He sits in a bare interview room, waiting—ten minutes, then twenty. Douglas Healy has pretty much seen it all, but the approaching sound of clanking and shuffling makes him stiffen in horror. Surely this shackled prisoner can't be fifteen-year-old Arjay Moran.

The hulking figure that appears in the doorway indeed looks very little like the average young teenager. He is a six-foot-five, 260-pound African American, built like a wrestler, with a barrel chest and huge arms that make his loose-fitting prison jumpsuit appear tight. Only his beardless face betrays his real age.

Healy stares at the shackles on the boy's arms and legs and the four guards who accompany him. Only Hannibal Lecter received more security. "Take those shackles off! I can't talk to someone who's chained like an animal!"

The oldest of the guards seems to be in charge. "No can do, Mr. Healy."

"He's a fifteen-year-old kid!"

"A fifteen-year-old kid convicted of manslaughter."

Healy turns to Arjay. "Is that really how it went down? You killed that guy?"

Arjay shrugs. "I hit him, and he didn't get up." Although his voice is low and rumbling, he speaks with an openness that's almost childlike.

"The report says he banged his head on a stone statue."

"Garibaldi," Arjay supplies blandly.

"So maybe it was an accident?" Healy prompts.

"Are you a lawyer?"

Remembering the meeting with Gecko, Healy asks, "Do you even know who I am?"

"You're the one who thinks he can get me out," the prisoner tells him.

"You don't seem excited by the idea."

It draws a snicker from the head guard. "This one—he isn't exactly what you'd call a live wire."

"In here, all anybody talks about is getting out," Arjay explains. "It doesn't happen very often."

"Well, this time it will." Healy lays out the same scenario that he presented to Gecko a few hours before.

Arjay has only one question. "Can I bring my guitar?"

Healy is blown away. Arjay Moran has just been offered a ticket out of hell, and the only thing he can think of is a *guitar*?

One of the younger guards speaks up. "You get used to the strumming after the first thousand hours."

"I like music," Healy announces. "Take the chains off."

Brilliant sunshine turns the choppy waters of Narragansett Bay to diamonds. It's a perfect New England scene—blue sky, whitecaps, even a family of seals basking on an outcropping of rock.

It means less than nothing to Terence Florian. He stands on the deck of the motor launch, never looking back at Lion's Head Island, where he has lived for the past seven months—or five hundred years, depending on whether you go by calendar time or how long it feels.

"You're an idiot," the counselors told him time and time again. "Lion's Head is one of the top alternative detention programs in the nation. There are thousands of applications for the spot we're wasting on you. Do you realize what life is like in a federal juvenile detention center? Those places are torture chambers compared to the way you live here."

Probably true—if you don't count the boredom.

Natural beauty? Try a useless rock in the middle of the ocean, too small for the seagulls to use as a poop target. Try milking cows, planting seeds, feeding chickens, and shoveling out barns. Try no TV for seven months, no contact with the outside world. For a Chicago kid, born and bred, it's like being exiled to the moon.

In his opinion, the only beauty in this ride is the fact that it's taking him away from Lion's Head. Where to? That's not important. He'll cross that bridge when he comes to it.

The terminus of the ferry service is a ratty ancient dock that's destined to sink into the ocean at any moment. Unfortunately, that doesn't happen today. It would be a great farewell to this dump.

Kellerman, the counselor, reaches out and hands him ashore.

"Grab your gear. We've got a long drive ahead."

Terence doesn't ask where they're heading. He's not giving Kellerman the satisfaction of knowing that he cares. He tosses his duffel in the back of the pickup truck. The biggest tragedy of his life so far isn't juvie; it's the fact that everything he owns in the world fits inside one little pack. Not that he's got big dreams; dreams are for suckers. His old man taught him that lesson fairly early on. The jerk never understood that while shouting, smacking, and cursing the dreams out of Terence, he was also giving Terence a dream of a different sort—the dream of putting several hundred miles between himself and his father. So far so good on that score.

He climbs onto the flatbed after his stuff.

Kellerman laughs mirthlessly. "Sure—I'm really going to let you ride back there. You'll be gone at the first bend in the road. You know the rules. Get in the front."

Terence isn't offended. He doesn't expect to be trusted. He's not trustworthy. "What do I care about the rules? What are you going to do—kick me out? I'm already kicked out." He grins. "Hey, Kellerman, what did I do, anyway? How come I got the boot?"

"You're kidding, right? You know the policy. Three strikes and you're out."

"That's the whole point," Terence persists. "I got

probably fifty strikes. What was so bad that it made even you guys give up on me? Or was it quantity, not quality?"

The counselor starts the engine and pulls onto the gravel access road. "Your new placement came through." He won't meet Terence's eyes.

Not a good sign, that. In spite of everything, Terence knows there are some pretty horrible whistle-stops on the juvie express. But he's determined to play it cool. "Whatever," he says with a yawn. For Terence, it's more than a word; it's a philosophy of life. If you've got it, you can survive equally at Alcatraz or Club Med.

Growing up with dear old Dad, if you make it past ten, you're a survivor.

He leans back in his seat and gazes idly out the window. Same old nothing, only now it's green instead of blue. And it goes on forever.

He breaks the long silence. "It was that state senator's visit, wasn't it? Like I was going to keep his stupid wallet. What was I going to spend it on, anyway?"

Kellerman shoots him a cockeyed glare. "So what was the point of taking it if it wasn't for the money?"

Terence shrugs. "Maybe *this* is the point. I'm out, right?"

The counselor sighs. "I know it's a waste of breath to tell you this, but a lot of us do what we do because we honestly want to help kids."

"Come to think of it," Terence muses, "it was

probably just the lobster in the toilet bowl." He's reasonably sure Kellerman turns away so he can smile.

He dozes off, and when he awakens, they're still nowhere, although the highway seems wider and busier. Then they round a bend, and there, on the horizon, is a vast city skyline.

For an instant, he wonders if they might have driven all the way to Chicago. But no. He recognizes the Empire State Building, the Chrysler Building—

"Is that *New York*?"

Kellerman keeps his eyes on the road.

"You're putting me in juvie in New York?"

"There's an experimental new program here. Just three boys."

Terence is astonished. "And they picked me? After the lobster thing?"

"Mr. Healy asked for you by name. Listen, Terence, I realize you never pay any attention to what I say, but hear me out: if your life isn't that terrible yet, it's only because you're the luckiest fool on the face of the earth. You just hit the lottery twice, and you don't even know it. There are only twelve placements on Lion's Head, and you frittered one of those away. Now you've been handed one of only three spots in this new setup. For God's sake, don't blow it!"

Terence makes no promises. Visions of the Big Apple are spinning in his head. Blow it? Maybe; maybe not. The important thing: there are definitely no cows in New York City.

CHAPTER FOUR

The apartment is on East Ninety-seventh Street—a narrow fourth-floor walk-up with peeling paint—cream over green over orange. It has to be the last place anyone would expect to find an installation of the United States Department of Juvenile Corrections.

Inside, the layout is tight and spare. There is a living room, a galley kitchen, and two bedrooms. The smaller of these is for Healy, the group leader. Two bunk beds and a single stand in the larger room, which the three teenagers are to share.

Gecko and Arjay moved in yesterday. Gecko is showing Terence the two dresser drawers that are reserved for him. But the new arrival is more interested in the fire escape that passes just outside the bedroom window.

"Don't even think about it," Gecko tells him. He raps on the heavy metal security gate locked over the opening. "Healy has the only key."

Terence looks at him pityingly. "You're kidding, right? I could have that key, and probably his underwear too, and he'd never know they're missing. I don't know about you guys, but I've been on a desert island for seven months. If I'm in New York City, I'm going to see more of it than the inside of this dump. Who's with me?"

Arjay sits on the single bed, picking at an acoustic guitar, which looks like a toy ukulele against his enormous frame. "Count me out," he drawls without glancing up. "I was at Disney World before this. I've had enough fun for a while."

Gecko regards Terence in surprise. "Didn't Healy give you the warning? That he had to fight to get this program going, and the whole thing is kind of a trial run? Mess up, and you go straight back into the system."

Terence dismisses this with a wave of his hand. "These do-gooders blow my mind. There's always somebody trying to save your soul—like that's going to happen."

Gecko sticks his jaw out. "Look, man, I came from a pretty bad place before here. I'm not doing anything to risk getting sent back."

The newcomer frowns at him. "Whoa, they put me in with the Boy Scouts by mistake! How'd you end up in the system? Get caught stealing merit badges?"

Gecko's face flushes red. "Is that how this works? I recite my rap sheet, and you recite yours, and we see who's the biggest gangster?"

Terence snorts. "Yeah, like *that's* up for grabs! Back in Chicago, my crew *owned* every block southeast of Evergreen! We ate solid citizens like you for breakfast!"

Gecko is surprised, and more than a little scared, by the intensity of the emotions roiling inside him. Terence's in-your-face arrogance is nothing new. Gecko has been taking this kind of crap from his brother since birth.

And how did I handle it? By not thinking while Reuben made me his getaway driver!

Not thinking with Reuben landed him in juvie. Not thinking with Terence will only get him shipped straight back there.

He peers into Terence's tough-guy sneer. His fist comes up, clenched and ready.

Healy and Kellerman sit at the small dining table, filling out Terence's transfer paperwork. There are forms from the federal government, the states of Rhode Island, New York, and Illinois, and the City of New York.

Healy sighs in frustration. "If anybody had paid this much attention to the kid *before* he got into trouble, he probably wouldn't have gotten into trouble at all."

"I hear you," Kellerman agrees. "Nobody ever lifts a finger to help them until they're in so deep that they can't be helped." He shoves a paper under Healy's nose for the final signature. "Tell me something—why are you doing this?"

Healy gives Kellerman his copies and sets aside his own for filing. "Same as you, probably. I want to give these kids a fighting chance."

The Lion's Head counselor shakes his head. "No. Then you'd get a job like mine. I can only imagine the kind of wheeling and dealing it must have taken to get approval for a special project like this. Not to mention a New Directions grant to help pay for it all. Why? What possibilities do you see here that are so different from a hundred other group homes and alternative setups?"

"The system is so vast," Healy explains, "that my contribution would disappear like spit in the ocean. But here I know I'm making a difference for three boys. It's only three, but it's definite."

"And why these three?" Kellerman persists.

Healy looks embarrassed. "That's a little more selfish. To tell you the truth, they remind me of me."

"How does the Incredible Hulk's kid brother remind you of you?"

The group leader appears haunted. "More than you could ever know. Arjay's the rarest thing in the system—a genuine innocent man. He just ran into a DA up for reelection in a bad year for youth crime."

"That happened to you?"

"Well, I didn't kill anybody, if that's what you mean. But I spent nearly three years in juvie for something that was an accident. An accident that never would have happened if I hadn't got mixed up with a crooked relative—like Gecko did."

The man from New England takes this in. "What about Terence?"

Healy's face clouds. "The system took a city kid and plunked him down in the middle of nowhere, a million miles from everything he knew. That was me, a native New Yorker. I sat on a farm in Nebraska, wondering where the sidewalks were."

Kellerman stands up. "When you put it that way, I can see why Terence wasn't very happy feeding chickens on the island."

Healy follows his visitor to the door. "How do you think he's going to do with me?"

"I'm sure he'll be just fine," the counselor replies, a little too glibly.

Healy stops him on the way out. "No, I want your honest professional assessment of my arrangement here."

Kellerman faces him. "I can't speak for the others. But the first chance he gets, Terence Florian is going to put a kitchen knife right between your shoulder blades."

On that note, he heads down the rickety stairs. The group leader watches him go, stunned by somewhat more honesty than he bargained for. And then the commotion reaches his ears.

He's across the living room and through the bedroom door in three frantic strides. The sight that meets his eyes is memorable. Arjay stands between the other two, straight-arming them apart. One ham-like hand is wrapped around Gecko's balled fist. The other is gripping the front of Terence's shirt.

Gecko's panting breath bubbles through his bloody nose. Terence is cursing through rapidly swelling lips. The nightstand has been upended, knocking a tall bowling trophy to the hardwood floor.

"What's going on?" Healy bellows.

Silence from Gecko and Terence.

Arjay says, "They slipped."

"That better be true, because fighting is one of the things that gets you kicked out of here!" Ruefully, the group leader picks up the fallen trophy. The metal figure of a bowler has snapped off the top, exposing the spike that held it in place.

Gecko reads the small brass plaque: CITY FINALS—1977; DOUGLAS HEALY—2ND PLACE. "Sorry," he mumbles.

Terence turns to Healy. "It's *your* trophy, man; what's it doing in *our* room?"

The group leader tries to replace the bowler on its pedestal. "It's the only thing I ever worked hard for when I was your age. I just thought—" The figure drops with a clatter. "Never mind. A little Krazy Glue and it'll be good as new."

Out the gated window, he can see Kellerman walking along Ninety-seventh Street to his truck. A shiver runs along Healy's spine.

Does he know something I don't?

CHAPTER FIVE

The Alma K. Walker High School is located on East Ninety-first Street, a ten-minute walk from the apartment. The stately old building's original three stories were built in 1867. The "new addition," the fourth and fifth floors, was constructed in 1912, shortly after the sinking of the *Titanic*.

Douglas Healy delivers his charges there the next morning. They are already preregistered, but the principal has requested what he calls an "orientation meeting." This consists primarily of chewing them out in advance for all the evil things they are probably going to do in his school.

They sit on the hard wooden bench and take it for a while. Finally, the group leader speaks up for them. "Dr. Cavendish—all due respect—I don't think this is fair. I'm not suggesting anyone should get special treatment, but none of these boys has so much as spit on the sidewalk."

"I did," pipes up Terence. The look he gets from Healy would melt steel.

The principal regards the group leader impatiently. "What's your point?"

"These are *my* kids. If you have any problems with them, you come to me. Pretend I'm their mother. Because, practically speaking, I am."

Dr. Cavendish either refuses to accept it, or is too dumb to understand it, because he concludes the interview with a warning: "I'm keeping my eye on you three. Expect a zero-tolerance policy here at Walker."

Healy leads them out of the office, and they stand in the hall, gathered around him.

"Thanks, Mom," Arjay intones.

Healy tries and fails to keep the corners of his mouth from turning up. Then he spots something that wipes all thought of smiling from his mind.

Gecko is alarmed. "You okay, Mr. Healy? You look like you've seen a ghost."

He has. And worse than that. Marching across the dark-stained terrazzo floor toward them is a woman built like a missile silo, her gunmetal-gray suit falling straight from the shoulders past a nonexistent waist.

"That's Ms. Vaughn!" he hisses. "She's the social worker in charge of our case!"

"We're golden," Terence says smoothly. "I'll just turn on the charm and—"

"Do *not* mess with that woman!" orders Healy through clenched teeth. "She fought me every inch of the way when I was setting up this program. She has the power to shut us down and send you guys back to lockup. And she's just looking for an excuse to do it!"

"Good morning, Mr. Healy. Boys. I was planning to stop by the apartment yesterday, but my caseload kept me hopping. The last thing I needed was another halfway house in my territory." Her expression implies that she has never uttered a kind word and isn't about to start now.

"Everything is great so far," Healy tells her. "The guys are really excited about starting their classes. In fact, they were just about to head to first period."

"And you have a plan in place for the end of the day?" Ms. Vaughn prompts.

"Absolutely," the group leader assures her. "We're meeting right outside the main entrance at three o'clock."

She nods briskly. "And they're aware that if they're not in your custody within fifteen minutes of dismissal that you are required by law to report them to the police as fleeing felons?"

"Right. They know all that—"

"*And* if they are unaccompanied more than one hundred feet from the building, they are subject to arrest?"

"Yes, they know that too."

"Excellent," Ms. Vaughn approves. "Then let's go to class."

The social worker plows through the crowded halls like an icebreaker, her Stonehenge-block heels resounding on the terrazzo. Dozens of probing gazes make the journey from Ms. Vaughn to the small party scrambling in her wake.

Connecting the dots, Gecko realizes. *If we're with the social worker, we must be social services cases. . . .*

Half an hour in the building, they're already being labeled and pigeonholed.

Terence picks up on it as well. "Man, too bad we can't take the witch with us everywhere! You can't buy this kind of cred!"

"Shhh!"

The first stop is a science lab, with students spread out at the experiment tables, heating up beakers of Pepto-Bismol–like pink liquid on Bunsen burners. Ms. Vaughn lingers just far enough inside the doorway for everybody to get an eyeful—the Problem Lady delivering her latest Problem.

The teacher, a youngish woman in a lab coat, looks at Gecko questioningly.

"Um—is this freshman chemistry?"

"You've got the right place. What can I do for you?"

Gecko hands over his course card.

"Oh," the teacher says dubiously, "a new student." The tables seem overcrowded already.

"I see you're fitting right in," announces Ms. Vaughn. "Have a nice day." She pounds away, leading Healy and the others.

The teacher files his course card in a drawer. "Everybody say hello to Graham."

"People usually call me Gecko." He's momentarily disconcerted by the whispered buzz, which churns out words like "foster home," "halfway house," and "juvie." It's an eerie reminder of walking into the mess hall at Atchison for the first time and having every inmate in the place size up the new guy.

The teacher musters a semblance of a smile. "Gecko it is. Go work with—" She scans the room. "Diego. Table six."

Diego is a small dark boy who tries to make himself even smaller at Gecko's approach. He shrinks turtlelike into his collar and backs away from the experiment as if it has suddenly grown fangs.

Gecko tries to put him at ease. "Okay, what are we doing? Bubbling up this pink stuff?"

Too frightened to speak, Diego merely nods.

They boil the solution away and smear the pink residue on a glass slide. The microscope is so old that it's impossible to see much. Gecko fiddles with the knobs for a long time before he realizes that he has focused on a reflection of his own eye.

Disgusted, he reaches for his notebook to cross out half a page of observations, but succeeds only in knocking the beaker off the counter. It shatters on the floor, showering pink sludge on the immaculate white sneakers of a kid working at the next table.

He's big, muscular, and very angry. "Hey, what the

hell?" He freezes at the sight of the offender, Gecko, the social services kid—possible gang member, possible felon, possible psychopath.

Gecko picks up a paper towel. "Let me clean that up for you."

"It's nothing!" the guy babbles. "Don't worry about it!" He wheels back to his own microscope and peers into the eyepiece with great concentration even though there's no slide on the tray.

Diego is beyond speech, as if he's just witnessed a terrible crime and is convinced that he'll be whacked to ensure his silence.

"I'm not a gangster," Gecko says coldly. "I drove the getaway car. When somebody gets run over, *then* you can be afraid of me."

Diego works up the courage to mumble his first-ever word to Gecko. "Sorry."

I might as well have stayed in jail, Gecko reflects bitterly. They may not beat you with soap here, but they still know how to hurt you.

It has been seven months since Terence Florian last set foot in a real school. For all intents and purposes, though, it's been a lot longer than that. Going to a school and going to school—attending classes, doing work, learning—are two very different things. He has no problem with being physically present in the building, but that's where his participation ends.

He knows the ropes. He's woven most of them.

The bathroom break, for one. With a little creativity, a twenty-five-second bodily function can be stretched into a twenty-five-minute absence from a forty-minute class. He takes one every period, which gives him a chance to cruise the hallways and scope the place out.

Everybody is always talking about big, bad New York City schools. This place isn't so tough. A cop on every floor. Big deal. His old school in Chicago was more heavily fortified than that secret warehouse in New Mexico where they keep the aliens in formaldehyde.

The footsteps are a dead giveaway. Cop shoes. The authorities would have a much better chance of sneaking up on people if they'd invest in a pair of New Balance.

A voice calls, "Hey—let's see your hall pass!"

It's invigorating to be chased again, although the pursuit is so lame that he can barely bring himself to speed up past a jog. He scampers down the stairs and ducks into a third-floor bathroom.

The stall doors have all been removed, and a business transaction is taking place in the end one. Terence surprises himself by recognizing the customer from one of the classes he briefly attended that day. The other kid has a dollar sign razor-cut into his very short hair. His shirt is rolled up to his belly button and about twenty cell phones are displayed in the high waistband of his boxers.

Spying Terence, the shopper shies away and rushes out of the bathroom. The seller whips down his shirt and begins nonchalantly washing his hands at the basin.

Terence is intrigued. "Nice merchandise. Cloned?"

It earns him a very angry frown. "Don't know what you're talking about, yo."

"The hardware. You jack it yourself, or are you in the middle?"

A lightning move, and a knife appears in the boy's hand. "Back off, dead man!"

And Terence does back off, beaming with something close to joy. He reverses out the bathroom door and punches the air in triumph. After seven months on that jerkwater island, he's finally found home again.

School might be the place for him after all.

CHAPTER SIX

The tiny office is above a take-out Chinese restaurant, up a dusty flight of stairs that smells of mothballs and fried rice. This is the nerve center of the Upper Second Avenue Business Improvement District. In addition to their school responsibilities, the three boys each owe the city of New York twelve hours per week of community service. Cleaning and sweeping this shopping area is how the city has decided they will serve their time.

The foreman, Jerry, is the most neatly dressed, well-groomed homeless person they've ever seen. He has gotten himself off the street working for the B.I.D. and now runs the place while still living in a shelter. He introduces them to the only other person on their crew today—a forty-three-year-old stock-broker paying off his own community service for a DUI conviction.

In the walk-in closet hang several dozen sets of

coveralls with the B.I.D. logo on the back. Gecko freezes with the pants halfway up his leg. They might call this a uniform, but it's really a jumpsuit, just like the inmates wear at Atchison. He promised himself not seventy-two hours ago that he'd never again put on one of these things.

His eyes meet Arjay's, and it's obvious that the big boy is struggling with the same thoughts. "Just a few yards of cotton," he reasons, trying to convince himself as much as Gecko.

Terence, who is as sensitive as a block of wood, shrugs himself right in. "Hey, guys—doesn't this remind you of lockup? Count off—one, two, three . . ."

He gets no appreciation from his intended audience, but the stockbroker guffaws loudly while zippering his coveralls over his three-thousand-dollar Armani suit. "Yeah, I get it. We look like a bunch of convicts, right? I should get a picture for the guys at the trading desk."

Grinning, Terence slaps him on the shoulder in a brotherly gesture, and they file from the closet change room.

Terence is halfway out the door when a big hand closes on the back of his collar.

"Hold up."

"Let go, man," Terence complains. "This is community service. Got to get out there and serve."

"Hand it over," Arjay orders sternly.

"What are you talking about? Hand what over?"

"That guy's wallet."

"You're bugging, Jumbo! I didn't jack anybody's wallet!"

Effortlessly, Arjay lifts Terence off the floor with one hand and begins patting him down with the other.

"Okay, okay—I'll give you half." His eyes take in Gecko. "Fine. Three-way split. The Three Musketeers, roommates to the end. What do you say?"

The big boy's expression darkens. "I don't care if you get yourself arrested and wind up on death row. But this gig is part of Healy's program, and that means it gets reported to Ms. Vaughn. And you know she's just looking for a reason to screw us. I'm not going back inside because you can't keep your hands off everything you see. The wallet. Now."

Petulantly, Terence hands it over.

"Hey, mister," calls Arjay, "you dropped your wallet."

Terence is thoroughly disgusted. "I'm surrounded by choirboys! What's the matter with you people?"

The three teenagers and the stockbroker are issued brooms and dustpans and sent out to rid Second Avenue of trash. It isn't hard work, yet somehow it's backbreaking to be constantly hunched over, peering into the gutter.

Gecko is amazed at what manages to find its way to a New York City sidewalk. The same square yard of pavement can be home to an apple core, a dead mouse, a six-year-old newspaper from Pakistan, the skeleton of what looks like an extinct fish, a Pez dispenser that resembles Adolf Hitler, and a tissue smeared with an unidentified teal substance that would surely glow in the dark.

The biggest problem isn't the garbage; it's the people. By four o'clock, the sidewalks are teeming with humanity. You lower your eyes to sweep up a coffee cup, and you're lucky if you don't get bodychecked into a parked car. Plus, more people bring more litter.

Terence works harder with his mouth than with his broom. "That's right! Throw another gum wrapper! You're a model citizen! Freak!"

Mostly, though, he takes endless bathroom breaks at the Starbucks on the corner.

The explosive roar of unmuffled engines cuts the air. Two souped-up cars on balloon tires erupt from the light and roar down Second Avenue, obviously drag racing. Gecko watches them till they're out of sight, almost overcome by the feeling of pure longing. He hasn't been behind the wheel of a car since he wrecked the Infiniti and got himself and his brother arrested. It is coming home to him that he will not drive again for a very long time.

Terence emerges from Starbucks after his ninth break and bats idly at a pigeon with his broom. Through the shifting sea of pedestrians, he spies a single pair of snake eyes watching him. The crowd parts to reveal the kid with the dollar sign razor-cut into the side of his scalp—the one moving cell phones from a waistband display.

Terence can't hold back a smile. Excellent. The jumpsuit and sweeper are as good as a military insignia in the language of the street. There are no saints on community service.

He's making an impression.

He looks over again, and the kid has disappeared.

At six thirty, Jerry, the homeless foreman, calls them back to the office to change out of coveralls and get their time sheets punched. Healy is waiting for them.

"They did great," Jerry assures him.

It's a compliment, Gecko reflects, but only on the surface. What it really says is that if these three halfway house convicts can get through a whole afternoon without killing anybody or soiling their uniforms, it's cause for celebration.

"I did some grocery shopping," Healy tells them on the way home. "We're having baked ziti and a tossed salad tonight."

"Man, I'm starving!" Terence exclaims. "Sure hope you can cook."

"Sure hope *you* can cook," Healy shoots right back. "I'm not your butler. Group home, group effort."

"Some mom you turned out to be," Arjay grumbles good-naturedly.

"Even in lockup they feed you," Terence argues. "They don't put you through the shredder all day and then expect more work when you get home."

"I'm glad you brought that up," Healy says mildly. "What you just described is called 'the real world.' Today can be your first life lesson. Don't forget to leave time for homework after we're done with the dishes."

They trudge up the concrete steps of their row house, and Healy lets them in the front door with its creaky hinges. For the first time, Gecko notices the doorbells, which are located above the mailboxes in the vestibule. Each buzzer is labeled with a name, but not 4B, which is covered by a strip of masking tape.

Halfway house means you only partially exist.

The narrow staircase is blocked by Mrs. Liebowitz, a frail elderly woman wrestling with two gigantic grocery bags.

Arjay jumps forward and takes one of the bags, reaching for the other.

The shriek that comes from Mrs. Liebowitz is like the mating call of a hawk. "Get away from me!"

Arjay jumps back as if he's been burned.

Healy speaks up. "It's okay, Mrs. Liebowitz. Arjay was just trying to help you. We all want to help you."

"You want to help me? Move your juvenile delinquents somewhere else! This used to be a nice building where you could borrow a cup of sugar from your neighbor without worrying if he's got a criminal record!"

The group leader tries to be kind. "I know you weren't pleased about accepting our program into the building. But now that we're here, I have to remind you that these boys haven't done anything to you. We're going to have to find a way to live together."

In answer, she snatches her bag back from Arjay, musters a hidden reserve of strength, and storms up the stairs without so much as a backward glance at her fourth-floor neighbors.

CHAPTER SEVEN

After all that Gecko has been through since flipping the Infiniti, this moment might be the most bizarre: sitting in a circle in a Park Avenue office while a punk rock girl lists her top ten ways to die.

". . . Number three," announces Casey Wagner with a tongue-stud lisp. "Space junk. There are hundreds of old satellites ready to drop out of decaying orbits onto some poor unsuspecting sap. Number two—radio waves from wireless devices. Hey, Wall Street guy, your BlackBerry is sterilizing my brain tissue!"

Terence adjusts the angle of his slouch on the uncomfortable chair. "What's number one? Being bored to death?"

"Terence," Dr. Avery warns sharply. "This is a safe environment. There's no interruption here. Go on, Casey."

Casey runs an agitated hand through blue-streaked spikes of her hair. "Well, it's a known fact that the island of Manhattan lies on a bigger earthquake fault than the San Andreas. One of these days, the George Washington Bridge is going to be a jump ramp."

Dr. Avery carefully straightens the jacket of her tailored suit. "Thank you, Casey. You've given us a lot to think about. Now here's something for you to consider: why would a young woman with her whole life ahead of her be so focused on death?"

"Isn't it obvious?" Casey gestures around the circle. "Look at us. Everybody's different. What's the one thing we have in common? We're all going to *die*."

Gecko holds his head. As if school and community service aren't enough, Social Services has decided the three boys need their heads shrunk. And that means their one free weekday afternoon is to be spent in Dr. Avery's adolescent psychotherapy group, which meets every Thursday at four.

It's a complete waste of what little spare time they have, but at least the scenery is good. Dr. Kathryn Avery is a drop-dead gorgeous blue-eyed blonde, with a supermodel figure not even her conservative business suit can conceal.

"You know, doc, I got fears too," Terence puts in. "Right now, I'm scared of leaving this office without your phone number."

There are snorts of laughter around the circle, and Casey bounces a crumpled piece of paper off Terence's forehead.

"For professional reasons!" Terence defends himself. "I'm a troubled youth. That's why I'm here."

"You're here because the court ordered it," Casey reminds him. "That's why we're *all* here."

"Mr. Healy has my emergency number," the therapist announces with a tolerant smile. "My service will forward any messages that can't wait."

"What, your *husband* doesn't like strange guys calling?" Terence takes in her ringless hand. "Or your boyfriend?"

The skin tightens a little on the supermodel cheekbones. "My personal life isn't what we talk about here."

"But you've got a boyfriend?" he persists.

"That subject is off-limits in this group."

"Wait a minute," Drew Roddenbury, a nerdy sixteen-year-old, speaks up. "You said *no* subject is ever off-limits in group therapy."

"I'm not a member of the group," Dr. Avery explains. "I'm here as a facilitator to make sure we have an open forum for everybody to express their feelings."

Terence nods at Drew. "Boyfriend. Definitely."

The therapist sighs. "Now, who else has something to share?"

Casey points to Arjay. "The big guy's ignoring me."

Arjay is blown away. "What did I do?"

"Sometimes it's hard to be new," Dr. Avery steps

in, "which might explain why we haven't heard much from Arjay and Graham."

"Gecko."

"Sorry—Gecko. What are your thoughts on joining our little group?"

"I'm not crazy just because I got arrested," Gecko tells her.

Her brow clouds. "We do not use that word in this room. We're all here because the court felt—"

"Get real, doc," Terence interrupts. "There's no way these cornballs ever saw the inside of a courtroom." He indicates the bestudded Casey. "Unless rivet-girl set off a metal detector somewhere."

"It wasn't the court, it was my truant officer," Casey replies coldly. "What's it to you? And Drew's a hacker. And Victoria's a klepto. Big whoop. At least we're not gangbangers like you."

Terence grins dangerously. He's always had more success as a thief and a B and E artist than as a tough guy. But it never hurts to pad your rep, even with losers like this bunch. "So what if I am?"

"Let's step back a moment," the therapist advises. "We want honesty, but we also have to respect one another."

"I'm not a hacker," Drew says into the silence that follows. "I just downloaded music off the Internet."

"No fooling." Arjay is interested. "I heard you could get in trouble for that, but I didn't think it ever really happened."

"The record companies sued me for copyright infringement, but they weren't interested in money. They just wanted to make an example of somebody. So they gave me a choice—pay them seventy-five thousand dollars or go into counseling."

Terence laughs out loud. "That's got to be the dumbest thing I ever heard! What did you download, man? I hope you're going through all this hassle for something decent."

"It was the Alan Parsons Project."

"The *what*?"

"They were big in the seventies," Drew explains. "It wasn't even for me. My brother made me download it for him."

In the entire hour of nonstop talking, it's the one comment that rings even the slightest bell with Gecko. He doesn't know much about falling satellites, but a kid who's in trouble for what his brother forced him to do—he can relate to that.

Given the chance, he knows he would switch places with Drew Roddenbury in a heartbeat. Then again, the way Gecko's life has been going, he'd probably be willing to switch places with anybody at all.

CHAPTER EIGHT

The band room is empty except for a lone figure on the front row of risers, hunched over an acoustic guitar. The opening notes of "Stairway to Heaven" fill the space. His calloused fingers move fluidly over the strings and frets by muscle memory.

Sure, it's a cliché—a teenager teaching himself guitar via Led Zeppelin's signature anthem. But during those fourteen horrible months behind bars, it was no cliché. At Remsenville, he played the song so many times, the guards called him Zep. During that endless night, music was the only thing that stood between Arjay and the void. He does not consider it an exaggeration to say "Stairway to Heaven" saved his life.

That and a rap sheet that says I killed a guy with one punch. . . .

Muscle memory deserts him, and he blows a chord as the image appears, unbidden, in his mind's eye.

Adam Hoffman. Quarterback. World-class idiot—

The tears come unexpectedly, and he blinks them back.

The Hawthorne Hawks couldn't handle the fact that the 260-pound freshman had no interest in trying out for football. It started with ribbing—weeks of it—and gradually turned ugly. Mob mentality—a team is a natural mob, trained to convert spirit into physical power. Anybody could see it was destined to come to a flash point. And it did—not at school, but on the way home, cutting through Cresthaven Park.

Badly outnumbered, Arjay fought back. He wasn't gunning for Adam; he wasn't gunning for anybody—although Adam was the loudest and most obnoxious. As a forest of arms grabbed him, Arjay balled a fist and let it fly. The impact was solid, but not overwhelming. Through the mass of bodies, he saw Adam topple.

Then . . . another crunch.

The trajectory of the quarterback's head changed suddenly. Adam dropped from view, revealing the statue—the gray stone hoof of Garibaldi's horse, stained red with blood.

Self-defense, a freak accident—was anything ever so obvious? But at the trial, the prosecution painted a very different picture. One by one, the Hawks took the stand, fearfully describing a high school murderer, an unstable fourteen-year-old in a strongman's body, with lethal weapons for arms.

A beloved local athlete brutally killed in front of his teammates and friends. The community must be protected from this monster. . . .

"We're losing," his lawyer told the Morans, urging Arjay to take a plea.

The man might as well have been speaking Swahili. Why would Arjay plead guilty when he was innocent? Wasn't that just plain wrong? The whole point of a trial was supposed to be getting to the truth. How could he lie?

Arjay wasn't a straight-A student or a Big Man on Campus, but he had complete confidence in his own judgment. Nobody could make him go out for a sport if he had no interest in it, just as no one could make him smoke or drink beer or shoplift or whatever the fashion of the nanosecond happened to be. And nobody was going to make him confess to murder when that wasn't what happened.

"We could get this kicked down to juvenile court," the lawyer argued. "As it stands, the prosecution wants to push for adult time."

The first mention of those fateful words: adult time.

If we knew then what we know now . . .

But would it have made any difference? He never would have copped when he was innocent. It went against the very core of his character.

By the end of the trial, his mom and dad looked like survivors from a besieged city—emaciated and drawn, haunted eyes peering from deep discolored trenches. The guilty verdict was almost a mercy for his parents, declawing their worst fears by realizing them. Anyway, there wasn't much mourning left in them by then.

And now? Sure, Mom and Dad are thrilled that he's out, but in a way, this is even harder on them. They can't call or e-mail or even write letters. For the next six months he might as well be dead.

Yesterday, he scribbled *Doing fine—don't worry* on a postcard of the Empire State Building and addressed it home. But he didn't have the courage to mail it. What if the Juvenile Corrections people were monitoring the Morans' mailbox? He's being paranoid, but fourteen months in Remsenville will make you that way. Absolutely nothing must jeopardize this chance to get his life back.

When the second guitar joins in, the counterpoint is so perfect that it takes a moment to process the fact that somebody else is in the room. A teacher stands in front of the risers, jamming with him. Arjay watches the man's fingers, fascinated. He's making it up as he goes along, yet it's all within the chord progression of "Stairway to Heaven," so the chaos sounds somehow right—a solo that pushes the envelope, but never goes too far.

Arjay launches into an ad-lib of his own, and the teacher retreats to the original. Now it's Arjay's turn to experiment, the pick just a blur in his hand.

They swing into the electric portion, the two guitarists strumming furiously in perfect unison. With a mischievous grin, the teacher increases the tempo, but Arjay catches up and powers ahead. The song falls apart there, degenerating into a blizzard of windmilling arms, and laughter.

The feeling is so alien that Arjay has to dig deep into memory to recognize it. He's having *fun*. He can't remember the last time.

The man puts down his guitar and holds out his hand. "Mr. Cantor, music teacher. Haven't seen you around here before."

Arjay shakes it. "I just registered last week. Arjay Moran."

"You're not in any of my classes. Where'd you learn to play like that?"

"I'm . . . self-taught."

"I've got a stage band here at Walker," Mr. Cantor tells him. "We do jazz, funk, a little bit of rock. I've been covering the guitar parts until we find a student, but you'd be a natural. We practice after school three days a week."

After school. There *is* no after school for Arjay; his free time consists of the fifteen-minute window between dismissal and the moment he officially becomes a fleeing felon. Not much of an opportunity for extracurricular activities.

Mr. Cantor reads the disappointment on his face. "Let me guess—after-school job, right?"

"Something like that."

"Any wiggle room on the hours?"

Arjay shakes his head sadly. Getting out of Remsenville was an advance on all the wiggle room he can ever expect in this life.

"Too bad," the music teacher says. "Well, Arjay, if your schedule opens up, you know where to find me. Good jamming with you."

Good. The word falls pathetically short of describing it. Playing alongside Mr. Cantor, Arjay felt like a human being again. At Remsenville, they treated him like a dangerous animal, but it isn't until now that he realizes how much he himself started to believe he was one.

"Same here. Thanks, Mr. Cantor."

Normal life is so close he can almost touch it. But when he tries, it turns out to be just beyond his reach.

CHAPTER NINE

Terence returns again and again to the third-floor boys' bathroom, but the cell phone salesman does not materialize. *Either the merch is all gone, or the kid has found someplace else to set up shop.* Or, Terence muses, Dollar Sign spends even less time in school than Terence would if he didn't have Healy breathing down his neck.

With more than four thousand students, Walker is larger than his old school in Chicago. You can't depend on running into somebody in the halls. He's been keeping an eye out, both in school and during community service. The kid is nowhere to be found. Did he get busted moving the phones? Somehow, he doesn't strike Terence as the careless type.

You've been wrong about people before, he reminds himself. And look how that turned out. . . .

His reverie is interrupted when he spots a familiar

razor-cut bobbing amid a sea of heads in the school foyer.

"Hey—" But he doesn't even know the guy's name. He wades into the jostling crowd in time to see his quarry walk out the double doors.

Terence follows, taking a moment to appreciate the strange sense of privacy that exists on the busy sidewalks of New York. So many people yet everybody minds his own business. Now *that's* beauty, not some jerkwater island.

Dollar Sign is across the street now, stepping into Falafel King for lunch. *What's falafel? Do they even have it in Chicago? No, scratch that. Who cares?*

Terence jaywalks and waits for the kid to emerge, munching on a pita sandwich.

Dollar Sign scans him with narrowed eyes. "Got a problem, yo?"

"Maybe I'm looking to buy a phone."

"Ever heard of the Home Shopping Channel?"

Terence grins appreciatively. "Want to show you something." From his pocket, he produces a video iPod, top of the line, mint condition.

"Birthday present from Grandma?" Dollar Sign asks in a bored tone.

"I've got a little community service gig with the B.I.D. This comes from a store by their office. Deep discount." He regards the boy intently. "Five finger."

"So?"

"So plenty more where this came from," Terence

goes on. "I think I might have a way in. . . ."

The fierce eyes flash. "What are you, some kind of cop?"

Terence laughs and holds out his hand. "Terence Florian."

"Hands to yourself, yo!" the kid snaps, and storms away.

Terence is triumphant. Only a potential conspirator avoids the appearance of conspiracy.

He follows at a distance. At last, Dollar Sign twists back into view. "Name's DeAndre."

Terence laughs. "Guess your mother went discount on the baby-naming book."

DeAndre's eyes widen in anger. For an instant, Terence is afraid he might go for his knife. All at once, the storm is over, and the kid is smiling at him. Teeth jagged, like a hammerhead shark's.

Terence presses his advantage. "Let me paint you a picture—big display of PS-3s stacked so high they block the motion sensor. You go in through the basement, stay in the shadow of the PlayStations, you're not even there."

DeAndre is intrigued, but he's also suspicious. "If you're messing with me, dead man, you picked the wrong yo."

Which only convinces Terence that he's picked exactly the right yo.

Gecko swipes his lunch card and scans the crowded

cafeteria. The absurdity of this daily gesture always gets to him. What does he expect to see? A table of buddies, waving and beckoning? He's an outsider here. An outsider pretty much everywhere, he realizes. Back home, high school has started, but without him. He's an MIA, a cautionary tale—*Keep your nose clean or you'll wind up like Gecko.* As for his family, he was always sort of a stepchild there. Mom, overworked, underpaid, struggling to make ends meet. Stressing over Reuben's life of crime left her little time to think about the other kid in the house.

His eyes fall on a familiar face—Diego from freshman chemistry, alone at a corner table.

Oh, right, like I'd be a welcome lunch guest there. The guy'll swallow his napkin when he sees me coming.

As Gecko watches, a furtive hand snakes down to Diego's lunch and applies a delicate flick to his plastic spoon, spraying soup in his face. When a shocked Diego wheels to investigate, an arm reaches around and dumps the contents of the tray into his lap. The freshman leaps up to confront his tormentor and finds himself face-to-chest with a tall, burly football type, Diego versus Goliath.

Gecko takes an instinctive step in his direction and freezes. *What am I doing? To Diego, I'm scarier than the kid who's picking on him.*

A mean-spirited bullying half-wit is still preferable to a convicted felon. Besides, it's not as if he and Diego are friends.

Anyway, the standoff defuses itself when Goliath is distracted by a table of cheering teammates. Gecko sets his own tray down at a spot by the window. It seems unfair that a total jerk has friends and he doesn't. Not that Gecko isn't grateful to be out of Atchison, but Healy's whole setup is like a guarantee against any kind of social life.

The food at Walker is pretty decent—compared to juvie, at least—but he can never seem to work up much of an appetite. He pushes his Salisbury steak away and peers through the dirty glass at the street scene outside.

To his surprise, he finds himself looking at Terence Florian. His roommate is on the opposite sidewalk, deep in conversation with a tough-looking kid Gecko has seen around school. Gecko frowns. The problem isn't Terence's choice of company; it's his location. Healy's trio is barred from venturing off campus during school hours. With the halfway house still on probation, any violation could shut it down.

I'm not going back to jail because of that idiot!

Lunch forgotten, he's out of the cafeteria, through the double doors, and darting past honking taxis.

Terence sees him coming. "Step off, dog. Private meeting."

"I'm not your dog!" Gecko hisses. "You know the rules—get back inside!"

DeAndre scowls over his falafel at the newcomer. "Who's your nanny?"

"Total stranger." Terence rakes Gecko with a severe gaze. "Right?"

Gecko doesn't budge. "Whatever you say—so long as you're saying it *inside*."

DeAndre takes a bite of his lunch. "I'll give you some time to get straight with the little yo." He begins an unhurried crossing of the street back toward school, forcing cars and buses to go around him.

Terence wheels on Gecko, furious. "You mess with my business again, I will *end* you!"

"You don't *have* a business!" Gecko fires back under tight control. "You have school, garbage picking, and therapy! That's your life!"

"You don't know squat about me!" Terence seethes.

"I know *everything* about you, man! My brother attracted puffed-up gangster wannabes like a magnet!"

"You want to waste your time being a good little worker ant, that's your dead end. Me, I've got plans."

Gecko looks him in the eye. "Not when your plans can get me locked up."

They're squared off, ready to do battle, when the supermarket door slides open, and Douglas Healy steps out behind two big bags of groceries.

Terence ducks into a storefront, but Gecko is fixed there like a butterfly on a pin.

"Gecko?" Plum tomatoes bounce from the bags as the group leader races up. "What are you doing, kid? You're not supposed to be here!"

"I—I know—" It never occurs to Gecko to explain himself—that he only left to bring Terence back in. The code of no ratting may belong to the Reubens and Terences of the world, but he can't bring himself to break it. "I messed up."

To his surprise, Healy's expression softens. "I did some time inside—in juvie, like you. Sometimes you need to feel the sun on your skin to remind you you're alive."

Gecko tries to look contrite, but all he feels is relief. This was a very close call. And with his fate tied to Terence Florian, the calls are only going to get closer.

CHAPTER TEN

Laundry night in the apartment on Ninety-seventh Street is Tuesday after community service. Arjay is carrying yet another overfilled basket to the basement washing machine when he finds his way blocked by a bag of garbage nearly as wide as the staircase. Frowning, he peers around the obstacle to find Mrs. Liebowitz backing gingerly down the steps, struggling with the awkward load.

Not my problem. The last time he tried to help this woman, she practically bit his head off.

But as he squeezes past the huge bundle onto the landing, he hesitates. The old lady can't even see her own shoes. She's going to fall and break her neck.

He sets down his basket and rips the big burden out of her arms. When she begins to protest, he silences her with eyes of flame.

He's most of the way to the next landing when she bursts out with: "You've got a lot of nerve—"

He cuts her off with another searing glare. Arjay is not a tough kid, but he didn't make it through fourteen months in Remsenville without developing the Look. Nonverbal communication is a vital survival skill in prison.

He squeezes through the front door and begins the arduous task of cramming the bag into one of the building's trash cans. Four floors up, Mrs. Liebowitz is grimacing down at him from her window.

He retrieves his basket and descends the musty flight to the basement. It's a claustrophobic place, especially for Arjay—low ceilings, flickering fluorescent lighting, and a pungent smell that combines mold and rotting fruit. But the atmosphere is pleasant compared with the looks he receives from Gecko and Terence.

"What?" he asks.

Gecko hands him a crumpled card. "It was in the pocket of your jeans."

He unfolds it. The Empire State Building. The postcard.

"And you're ragging on *me* for taking risks?" Terence accuses.

"No contact with our families for six months," Gecko adds.

Arjay studies his sneakers. "I didn't have the guts to mail it. It's just hard. At least in jail, your folks can visit you. This is like we've dropped off the face of the earth!"

Terence is unmoved. "Nobody visited *me*, dog. Course, I wasn't exactly centrally located. But if I was doing my time in our toilet bowl, my old man wouldn't have bothered to lift the seat to check on me."

"I was only at Atchison for a couple of months," Gecko puts in. "My mom would have gotten around to me. My brother's in a worse place, so she focuses on him."

"To hell with them all, man," Terence says bitterly. "You turn on the TV, you see these families all lovey-dovey and supportive. Science fiction. Your only friends are your dogs. A solid crew, that's money."

Gecko bristles. "Just because you've got problems with your old man doesn't mean my family's like that. My mom works three jobs. She's got a lot on her mind."

Arjay steps between them. "Don't you guys start anything because of my screwup." He tears the postcard into tiny shreds over the garbage can. "See—it's finished. No harm done."

As they stuff the machine for a final load, it occurs to Arjay that he's the only one with a home to miss. Terence wants nothing to do with his family, and Gecko seems all but abandoned by his. The painful surprise is that Arjay is actually at a *disadvantage* because he comes from a great mom and dad. The others just have to feel sorry for themselves. He has to agonize over his parents too.

* * *

Victoria Ko is sporting a glittering sterling silver and marcasite necklace that she definitely wasn't wearing at last week's group therapy session.

It does not escape the luminous blue eyes of Dr. Avery. "It's lovely," she says carefully. "Where did you—get it?"

"You like?" The girl cranes her neck, modeling. "It's from the jewelry counter at Bergdorf's."

Casey is disgusted. "She means how did you take it out of Bergdorf's? In a bag with a sales slip or stuffed inside your bra?"

"So she boosted it, so what?" Terence says with a yawn. "It's like the stuff's just sitting there, begging to be jacked."

Arjay delivers a sharp wallop of warning to the back of his head.

"It's cool," Terence assures him. "Doctor-patient privilege—inadmissible in court. You can spill your guts. You can even talk about that kid you whacked."

Arjay's neck muscles bulge, but his response is measured, quiet. "You don't know what you're talking about."

Terence shrugs. "No lock on Healy's filing cabinet. I know you and your dog Garibaldi took out somebody. I'm down with that. Back in Chicago, my crew—"

"Garibaldi isn't my 'dog,' you idiot!" Arjay seethes under tight control. "It's the statue the guy hit his head on! It was an *accident*."

Dr. Avery moves quickly to steer the subject in a different direction. "All right, Terence. What were you going to say about your 'crew'?"

"Just that we had it going on," Terence replies in a subdued tone. "Nobody messed with us, not even the cops."

"Yet you got arrested."

A shrug. "It happens."

Casey speaks up. "All I did was cut school, and they've got me with killers and gang leaders and . . ." Her black-polished fingernail stops at Gecko.

"I drove without a license," Gecko supplies.

"Yeah," snorts Terence, "in a stolen car full of swag."

"I just drove," Gecko says stubbornly. "What and where, blame *that* on my brother."

"Why?" Anita seems genuinely confused. "If you drove the car, what does your brother have to do with it?"

Drew is cluing in. "He's the one who stole it, right? He stole the car and *made* you drive it, just like *my* brother—"

"It's a totally different thing," Gecko interrupts irritably. "You think Reuben's heard of the Alan Whatsisface Project? He doesn't even like music—except to make me dance to his tune."

"So what does that say to you?" interjects Dr. Avery.

"I don't want to talk about it," Gecko mutters.

"Your boyfriend's off-limits? Fine. My brother is too."

"Your brother," snorts Casey. "More like your *crutch*. Must be nice to have a built-in scapegoat so you can cry 'no fair' when you get what you deserve."

Arjay's voice is quiet. "Maybe you should spend some time behind bars before telling us what people deserve."

"Let's take a moment," Dr. Avery advises.

But Casey's point is not lost on Gecko. Is that what his not thinking is all about? Did he let Reuben push him around so that, no matter what happened, it would be his brother's fault?

He remembers that fateful vacation—Gecko, age nine, behind the wheel of the go-kart, burning up the boardwalk track. Even as a little kid, he couldn't miss the lightbulb going off above teenage Reuben's head. Some part of him has always understood that his brother was molding and shaping the ultimate getaway driver. But not thinking kept the notion buried.

Was it just because I never had the guts to stand up to Reuben?

Or could it be what Casey said—a crutch, an excuse to keep doing the illegal thing he loved, while laying the blame on somebody else?

Gecko glowers at the punk rock girl. Right or wrong, she definitely has a point about one thing: truancy, downloading music, petty shoplifting—in the eyes of the world, Casey, Drew, and Victoria are regular teens who need a little therapeutic help over the rough terrain of adolescence. Gecko, Arjay, and Terence, by contrast, are hard-core criminals.

It'll take a lot more than a supermodel shrink to bridge that chasm.

The mood is sour when Healy collects them in the lobby.

The group leader immediately senses that something is not right. "Out with it," he prompts as they head north on Third Avenue. "What happened?"

Gecko is generally depressed, but Arjay has a specific grievance. "Ever hear of keeping your mouth shut?" he growls at Terence. "You should try it sometime. It's a wonderful hobby."

"Bite me," Terence retorts irritably.

"It's therapy," Healy reminds them. "It's going to get personal, and there will be days that you walk out of that room ticked off at each other. Deal with it. We still have to live together."

"You're not the one with your guts under a microscope," Arjay mumbles.

"Been there, done that," Healy replies honestly. "Cheer up, guys. Your luck is about to change. Look what I got us for dinner tonight." He reaches into a plastic bag and pulls out a large crusty loaf, covered in seeds.

Terence is skeptical. "Bread and water again?"

"None of you Philistines grew up in the city, so I'll forgive your ignorance. This, gentlemen, is a caraway rye from Schnitlick's bakery. People come all the way from Pennsylvania for one of these. I've got some cold cuts at home. You never had it so good."

Arjay frowns at the oblong slab. "I don't know whether to eat it or punt it."

"Have it your way—" Healy grasps the loaf like a football and fire passes it into Arjay's chest.

The big boy is so shocked that he barely manages to close his arms around it. "Jeez, Mr. Healy."

The group leader snatches it back and pantomimes a quarterback's three-step drop. "Terence—go long!"

"Forget it, man—"

But the rye is already in the air. Terence leaps, getting his fingertips on the shrink-wrap and gathering in the package. Grinning mischievously, he rears back and flings the loaf at Healy's face. The group leader snatches it out of the air a split second before it would have taken his head off.

Healy cackles in triumph. "All right, Gecko, your turn!" And the bread is headed his way.

He catches it and tosses it carefully back. The three boys are not quite sure what to make of this easy playfulness. Gecko spent his childhood tiptoeing around the Wrath of Reuben, and fun has never fit into the street reputation Terence is always trying to cultivate. As for Arjay—he's not a football fan, and for good reason. His life has been in free fall ever since the Hawthorne Hawks tried to recruit him.

Yet there's Healy, laughing and shouting with an infectious enthusiasm. It doesn't seem to bother him at all when their dinner gets bounced off walls and pavement—not even when it rolls into the road and is narrowly missed by a double-decker sightseeing bus.

The avenue is crowded, but when they turn the corner onto Ninety-seventh, the "game" opens considerably. Arjay palms the rye in his massive hand, determined to expiate his football demons with one long bomb.

The receivers, Healy included, take off down the block, and the big boy launches a Hail Mary.

Gecko glances over his shoulder and spies the pass arcing high over the streetlights.

"Heads up!" Arjay shouts.

There is a thump followed by a cry of shock as the projectile bounces off the figure of a large woman standing in front of their building.

Gecko rushes up and scoops the dented rye off the sidewalk. "Sorry, lady—"

A wheeze comes from Healy that has nothing to do with his forty-yard sprint.

It's Ms. Vaughn.

The social worker's expression changes from dismay to rage. "Mr. Healy! What on earth—?"

The group leader is a sight to behold, dripping sweat, face flushed, panting with exertion. "Sorry, Ms. Vaughn. We didn't mean to hit anybody."

"Why are you hurling food around at all?"

Healy looks sheepish. "The boys seemed kind of down. I thought a little fun might cheer them up." He notices Mrs. Liebowitz watching from the stoop, taking it all in. It's like being in a foxhole, surrounded by enemies.

"They don't need cheering up. They need to be contained." Ms. Vaughn's face, never friendly, grows creased with disapproval. "I don't have to remind you that they're all convicted felons, who could be scattering to the four winds while you catch your breath. This is not going to look good in my report."

"Scattering?" pants Terence. "I've barely got the strength left for a nap."

A terrified Arjay jogs up behind him.

Healy takes another stab at explanation. "Rehabilitation is a tough road. These kids have a better chance of making it if there are a few pleasant moments in their lives."

She's unmoved. "Rehabilitation is your *second* priority. Your first is protecting the general public. These boys are volatile enough without you encouraging them to be wild. I haven't even set foot inside the apartment, and already I've caught you committing numerous violations and endangering the public safety."

"Hey, man," Terence wisecracks, "if the bread's not pressing charges—"

Arjay puts a chummy arm around his shoulders and squeezes hard enough to crush bone.

The social worker glances impatiently at her watch. "Well, let's get on with it. I have other drop-ins scheduled—too many, as matter of fact. And rest assured that every unwashed sock and speck of dust will be duly noted."

Squaring her ample shoulders, she marches up the steps to the front door, Healy and his charges following meekly behind. They receive the usual scowl from Mrs. Liebowitz. As Healy lets them in, their neighbor pulls Ms. Vaughn aside.

Now, here's the cherry on the bitter ice-cream sundae, Gecko reflects. Visions of a return to Atchison swim before his eyes. They all know exactly the kind of character witness Mrs. Liebowitz is going to be.

"I'm guessing that you never raised children," the elderly woman tells her. "You should be worrying about keeping them from harming innocent people, not about dirty socks. That's a waste of your time and my tax dollars."

The three teenagers exchange meaningful looks. When it comes to sheer nastiness, Ms. Vaughn still has a few things to learn from Mrs. Liebowitz.

And here we are, thinks Gecko, caught in the crossfire.

CHAPTER ELEVEN

There's no such thing as total darkness in Manhattan. The glow of the city creeps into even the most isolated alley and air shaft. Light coming through the steel window grille projects bars on the wall beside Terence's lower bunk, a jailhouse image.

No, not just an image. It *is* jail. The grate's purpose is to keep intruders out, but here it's serving to keep the inmates *in*. The only other exit is the front door, and that's a dead end. Healy alone knows the alarm code.

It's a solid setup, security-wise—except that, clutched in Terence's fist as he lies in bed, waiting, is the key to the grille.

He's gratified to hear deep, even breathing from Arjay, and nothing at all from Gecko, who's normally such a restless sleeper that he kicks up a constant rustle. From the smaller bedroom, Healy's buzz-saw snoring, which often keeps them awake, is unmistakable.

The nightstand clock reads 12:37. His meeting with DeAndre is scheduled for one a.m. in the alley beside the electronics store.

DeAndre. Just the thought of his razor-cut dollar sign brings a smile to Terence's lips. Now, there's an individual who recognizes a business opportunity. Not like those hayseeds back in Chicago. They never appreciated what Terence had to offer. But New York, New York—like the song says, if you can make it here, you can make it anywhere. He and DeAndre are going to own this town, and it all starts tonight.

Silently, he creeps out of bed, shrugs into jeans and a sweatshirt, and scuffs into sneakers.

The key is a perfect fit and turns without a sound. The grille is another story. Stiff from age and lack of use, the hinges squeak sharply as it slides open. He freezes, senses alert, like a rabbit under attack. His roommates are still out. The coast is clear. He raises the window. More noise—the groan of metal on metal.

And then it's done. He ducks through the opening and finds himself on the ancient slats of the fire escape. Adrenaline surges through his body as he starts down the steps. There's nothing quite like the thrill of making a move.

He's passing the third-floor landing when he's grabbed from behind. "Where are you going?" It's Gecko, always in the wrong place at the wrong time.

"Mind your own business!"

"No!" Gecko rasps.

"I'll be back in an hour!"

"You'll be back *now*." Another hand closes on Terence's shoulder. A very large hand that will not shake off so easily.

"This has nothing to do with you," Terence pleads with Arjay. "I've got to meet a guy!" There seems to be no talking his way out of this standoff. He takes stock of his options. He could make mincemeat out of Gecko, but the big dog?

Terence shoves Gecko with all his strength into Arjay and twists away, his frantic footfalls ringing on the iron steps. Gecko grabs him around the waist and jams him against the railing. Arjay tries to wade into the fray, but Terence kicks at him with flailing sneakers.

"*Hey—!*"

The combatants look up. Healy is at the window, groggy, astonished, and angry, all at once.

Gecko punches at Terence. "Now look what you've done!"

"If you'd left me alone, he'd still be asleep!" Terence snarls back.

Healy is on the fire escape now, dressed only in T-shirt and gym shorts, barefoot on the metal stairs. "Don't move a muscle, you guys!"

Terence struggles to free himself, but Arjay has a hold on his wrist tight enough to pulverize it.

"Let's get out of here!" Terence urges.

"No!" Arjay cuts him off.

"We go with Healy *now*, we're back in juvie!"

"Shut up!"

The group leader is just a few steps away. Terence knows he can't outmuscle Arjay, but if there's one thing the streets of Chicago taught him, it's how to fight dirty. He launches himself at the much larger boy, driving his head with crushing force into Arjay's chin. The impact sends Arjay sprawling backward right into Healy, knocking him up and over the rail. With a cry of shock, the group leader plunges three stories into the garbage cans below.

"Mr. Healy!" Gecko gasps, leading the stampede down the fire escape.

With a superhuman burst of strength, he yanks on the lever that lowers the ladder to street level. The clatter of the wrought-iron extension screeching into place is earsplitting enough to rouse half the city, but Gecko can't think beyond the group leader. He scrambles to the bottom and jumps to the pavement beside Healy, who lies flat on his back amid the wreckage of the trash, unmoving and unconscious. A puddle of blood widens on the concrete around his head, a dark halo.

"He's dead! He's dead! He's dead! He's—"

Arjay drops to the pavement. He wants to quiet Gecko, but the sight of the group leader sucks the air from his lungs and convulses him with dry heaves. It's Adam Hoffman all over again. "Oh, God—"

"Shut up, man, you want the cops on our necks?"

Terence hops down and bends low over the victim. "He's alive!"

Hope soars in Gecko's heart. Terence is right. Healy is still breathing. His chest rises and falls almost imperceptibly.

"Mr. Healy," he says softly.

"Don't wake him, genius," says Terence. "The first thing he'll do is call the police."

Arjay snaps his fingers twice in front of the group leader's chin. "He's not waking so fast. He's really messed up."

"We have to take him to the hospital!" Gecko exclaims.

"Do you *want* to go back to jail, or are you just stupid?" Terence demands. "We take him in, we're busted!"

"It was an accident!" Arjay insists.

"Think the cops'll buy that from *us*?"

Gecko and Arjay exchange a look in the city gloom. As angry as they are at Terence, they recognize the truth of his words. When three felons show up with an injured man, the authorities will assume *they* did the injuring. Arjay has already bet and lost on an "accident" defense. He's in no hurry to try it again.

Gecko's eyes widen in disbelief. "So we just *leave* him here?"

"You think I feel great about it?" Terence demands. "Maybe we can move him where he'll get noticed. Someone'll call for help—"

"He's going to the hospital," Arjay says firmly.

Terence wheels on him. "You're not listening, man—"

A vein bulges on the big boy's forehead. "Either *he* goes, or *you* do!"

Terence backs off, but he doesn't back down. "How do we get him there, huh? Dial nine-one-one and we've got the NYPD on our necks!"

Gecko turns to Terence. "Do you know how to hotwire a car?"

Arjay perks up. "Drive him ourselves?"

Gecko nods. "And then take off."

"The cops could still follow us," Terence points out.

"They can try," says Gecko Fosse.

CHAPTER TWELVE

Healy doesn't move or make a sound as Gecko and Arjay wrap a towel around his head. The trickles of blood from the nose and ears have stopped, but the wound at the back of the skull is still oozing.

At the curb, Terence is working with a flathead screwdriver on the lock of an old Toyota Camry, jamming and twisting vigorously. For all the stolen vehicles Gecko has driven for Reuben and company, this is the first time he's ever witnessed the procedure firsthand. He's amazed at how quickly Terence is inside the car, prying open the steering column with the flathead. Still, it can't be fast enough for Gecko, not under the circumstances.

Hang in there, Mr. Healy!

There's a roar as the engine catches.

Arjay takes hold of the patient under the arms, while Gecko lifts by the ankles. It's like carrying an inanimate object, a dead weight.

No, not dead. Not yet . . .

Terence rushes over to help, supporting the torso from underneath. Together, the three of them manage to lay Healy across the rear seat. Terence tries to make his escape then, but Arjay horse-collars him and stuffs him in with the group leader.

"I'm late for a meeting," he complains. "Besides, there's no room—" He pulls back a split second before Arjay slams the door shut on his face. Gecko clicks the child locks.

The rush is familiar to Gecko—*I'm driving again!* But nothing can erase the tragedy on the fire escape. "Where's the hospital?"

Arjay's eyes widen. "You don't know?"

"We're not allowed a hundred feet from school! You think I've done the grand tour?"

Terence lowers the window. "Hey!" It's almost one a.m., but the avenue is busy. "Where's the nearest hospital around here?"

Eventually, someone directs them to Yorkville Medical Center on Lexington Avenue and Eighty-seventh Street. Gecko swings the Camry across four lanes of traffic, drawing a cascade of angry horns. A truck pulls away from the curb directly into their path. Gecko stomps on the brakes, and they lurch to a halt inches from collision. Healy's unconscious body tumbles off the seat onto Terence.

Shock, followed by revulsion. "Aw, man, he's bleeding on me!"

Arjay twists around to help push the patient back onto the seat. “That’s good news. Dead men don’t bleed.”

Never before, Gecko is certain, has anyone coaxed such speed out of a Toyota Camry. The sedan hurtles across Ninety-sixth Street to Lexington. They run a red light, shooting the gap between two accordion buses, and roar downtown in the fire lane.

The street signs fly by: Ninety-first . . . Ninetieth . . . Eighty-ninth . . . There it is—Yorkville Medical Center. He aims the Camry up the circular drive to the overhang marked EMERGENCY.

The trio hoists Healy out of the backseat. The automatic doors slide open with a whoosh that nearly startles them into dropping him.

“Leave him outside,” hisses Terence. “I’ll make sure they know he’s here.”

They prop Healy gently against the wall. Hiding his face behind a hand, Terence pokes his head into the emergency room and bellows, *“Oh, my God, he’s bleeding!”* and dives in the open rear door of the Camry.

As they peel away, an ambulance howls up the drive, blocking them in. Gecko shifts into reverse and stomps on the accelerator. The peace of Lexington Avenue is shattered by a cacophony of angry horns as the Camry powers backward into moving traffic. Taxis whiz past on both sides; enraged drivers shout and shake their fists.

Gecko throws the Toyota into drive, and they catch up with the flow of vehicles. He checks the mirror for signs of pursuit. So far so good.

Terence pulls a leather wallet from his pocket and rifles through it listlessly, plucking out cash and credit cards. He unfolds a crumpled slip of paper and examines it in dismay. "Figures—the alarm code. If we'd had this an hour ago, nobody would have set foot on that fire escape."

Gecko is appalled. "That's Healy's wallet? We're racing to save his life, and you're *robbing* the guy?"

Terence looks disgusted. "Fine, we'll just max his plastic with cash advances."

"It's not enough to toss him off a building!" Gecko seethes.

"Credit card fraud, man! He won't have to pay! And we need the dollars to get out of town!"

"Who said anything about leaving?" Arjay puts in.

"Think I'm thrilled about it?" Terence retorts sourly. "I'm the only one who appreciates this place! But it's nuts to hang around the jurisdiction now."

"We're federal prisoners," Arjay reminds him. "The whole country is our jurisdiction. If we try to run, they'll find us. Maybe not today, or tomorrow, but sooner or later."

"You talk like we've got a choice," Terence says bitterly.

"Healy was trying to help us," Arjay points out. "Maybe he still will."

"Doesn't matter!" Terence explodes. "Whatever Healy was doing, it's busted. What's the first thing he's going to say when he wakes up? 'Where are the guys?' And then a whole lot of men in blue will come knocking on our door."

"Yeah, but Healy knows that too," Arjay reasons. "Sure he's mad, but if he spills the beans, everything he worked for is gone. So he phones the apartment. We answer. We apologize like crazy and promise not to move a muscle until he gets home. Tomorrow morning, he gets released, and life goes on."

Gecko stops the car in a yowl of burning rubber. The three of them stare at one another for a long moment.

Terence is the first to find his voice. "You're no murderer," he tells Arjay. "Only an innocent man could dream up a plan like that."

"Do you think it could work?" Gecko asks anxiously.

"Only if we all stick together," Arjay tells him. "If one of us disappears, there'll be an investigation. Then we'll never keep tonight a secret." He looks pointedly at the backseat passenger.

Terence sighs. "I'm in. God, I'll try anything once."

The Camry's original parking space has already been taken, so they ditch the car in the nearest open spot. Gecko works at some of the bloodstains using a package of Wet Ones from the glove compartment, with limited success. The wreckage of the Infiniti is on his mind as he scrubs. Caught in the firestorm unleashed by that accident, there was never time to apologize for messing up a really nice car.

There's always so much to be sorry for . . .

"We should go," Arjay urges. "Healy could be calling any minute."

Their building is blessedly quiet. No squad cars cordon off the block. No police line tape surrounds the upended trash cans where Healy fell. They go in the same way they went out—via the fire escape. Arjay hauls the heavy access ladder back into place. They are covering their tracks, setting everything right again. Yet one of their number is missing in action.

The apartment is just as they've left it, yet it feels as alien as a biosphere on Mars. In their New York life, Healy was everything. Nothing can be the same without him.

The phone sits silent atop the TV cabinet next to the repaired bowling trophy. The message light is not flashing.

The waiting begins. An hour. Two hours. Three.

Arjay gets up to go to the bathroom, and his heavy footsteps jar loose the glued-on figure of the bowler, which clatters to the floor. In the four a.m. quiet, the noise is a bomb blast.

Terence jumps to his feet. "That pizza place on Third is twenty-four hours. Who's hungry?" He plucks a few bills out of Healy's wallet on the table.

"That's not your money!" Gecko tells him.

"Why do you think Healy gets those government checks?" Terence argues. "To feed us."

The front-door alarm is the next hurdle. Arjay punches the code into the keypad. There's a beep, and the system disarms. Finally, something has gone right. It's hard to remember the last time.

"I'll be back," Terence promises.

Gecko is not convinced, and says so.

Arjay shrugs. "He's got nowhere to go."

Still, when the boy from Chicago returns forty minutes later, the relief in the apartment is palpable.

Terence picks up on the vibe. "You thought I was going to blow." He sets the pizza box on the kitchen table. "Thought so myself for a while."

The steaming pie sits untouched. Everyone is starving; no one has an appetite.

Five a.m. Gecko asks the question that's on everyone's mind. "What if Healy doesn't call?" He doesn't say what his brain won't stop screaming: *What if he's dead?* There are other possibilities. He could still be unconscious. He could have no access to a phone.

Or he could be dead. Please, God, don't let him be dead!

Arjay thinks it over. "Our plan was to act like everything's normal. That's still on."

"You mean go to school?" Gecko asks.

Terence makes a face. "I hardly ever went to school when my old man chased me down the street with a shovel. You expect me to go *voluntarily*?"

"If we ditch, it gets reported to Ms. Vaughn," Arjay points out. "She may be the least of our problems now, but she can still put us behind bars."

"What about garbage picking and therapy?" Terence stares at the big boy. "Not those too?"

Arjay sucks in a deep breath. "Let's hope it doesn't come to that. For all we know, Healy's on his way home right now. But until he's back, we're obedient little robots, doing everything we're programmed to."

CHAPTER THIRTEEN

The students of freshman chemistry gradually get used to Gecko. Even Diego advances to the point where he can talk to his lab partner without having to physically hold down his breakfast. Gecko doesn't blame him for his meek personality. The poor kid seems to have a reputation as a target among some of the older jocks at school. He lives in constant fear of being used as a punching bag by a gaggle of Neanderthals. Small wonder he didn't jump for joy at the prospect of working alongside a Social Services case. For all he knew, Gecko would be even worse.

Gecko is sympathetic, but he's got problems of his own to worry about. Starting today, he's technically a fugitive. No Healy, no custody. From a legal standpoint, he's an escaped convict, and that changes everything. The familiar halls of Walker High suddenly seem alien. The whole city does. New York is the same, but everything is different about Gecko's place there.

"Diego," calls the teacher. "Do me a favor? I need you to run down and ask the custodian for more paradichlorobenzene."

Diego turns pale, and Gecko understands why. The custodian's office is by the gym, right smack in the middle of the phys ed wing. For Diego, that's like a walk through hostile territory with a bull's-eye on his forehead.

"I'll go," Gecko volunteers. It's not as if he's learning anything today. So far, his fevered brain hasn't conjured up a single thought that isn't of Douglas Healy.

Diego regards him gratefully.

"Thanks," the teacher tells him. "Ask for mothballs."

"Mothballs?" Gecko repeats. "I though you wanted para—" His tongue twists.

"Mothballs *are* paradichlorobenzene," she explains.

"Typical," Diego grumbles, making notes. "They pretend we're learning high-level science, and—" He looks up to see his lab partner dashing out the classroom door.

Gecko has made a split-second decision. Freshman chemistry will have to wait for its paradichlorobenzene.

He's on his way to Yorkville Medical Center.

* * *

"I'm here to see my uncle," he tells the receptionist. "Douglas Healy."

"Healy—H-E-A?" Long fingernails click at a keyboard. "I don't see anything. Are you sure you've got the right hospital? Metropolitan and Mount Sinai aren't too far away."

"No, definitely here." Gecko struggles to appear calm. "He—uh—arrived at Emergency around one a.m."

The nails are just a blur. "It's unlikely he'd still be in the ER. What was the nature of the complaint?"

Gecko hesitates. "He was—bleeding."

She tries to be kind. "You're going to have to be a little more specific than that, honey."

"His head was bleeding. He fell."

The clicking accelerates. "Our head trauma unit is on Seven East. I don't see your uncle listed, but they could have entered his name wrong—or not at all, if he just transferred up there."

"Thanks."

Gecko's imagination runs wild all the way to the seventh floor. Does this mean Healy's dead? Is that why he isn't in the computer?

Nightmare scenarios roil his thoughts as he stands in a crowded waiting area between the two banks of elevators. Hospital personnel in scrubs bustle by, waving ID badges in front of door scanners. There are intercoms for visitors, but Gecko doesn't feel much like explaining his reason for being there.

What can he tell them—that he's come to see a nonexistent patient?

He ponders his options for a few precious minutes. Back at school, study hall has already begun. He's due in English in half an hour, and he still owes freshman chemistry a box of mothballs.

If I'm going to do this, it has to be now. . . .

An entire extended family pours out of the elevator, jabbering excitedly in a language Gecko doesn't recognize. The mom gets on the intercom, struggling to communicate in broken English.

"Slow down, ma'am," comes the voice of the duty nurse. "Who exactly are you trying to see?"

The question only stokes the woman's agitation, accelerating her speech pattern.

"Slower, ma'am, I can't understand you—ma'am?" Finally, the door buzzes open.

Gecko knows he'll never get a better chance than this. He darts over and joins the swarming family members. The door closes behind him.

I'm in!

He sticks close to the family partway down the corridor and then breaks away, peering into patient rooms.

He rushes from door to door along the hall, taking a quick inventory of the occupants. *Twenty-five minutes to English.* Even sprinting, school is a good ten minutes away.

Come on, Mr. Healy, where are you?

Dozens of rooms, four beds a pop. No sign of the group leader. There's a parallel hall on the opposite end, but the only way to get there crosses right in front of the nurses' station. Locking his eyes straight ahead, he marches past the desk and starts his reconnaissance on the other side. These rooms are smaller, with two beds in each. All are occupied, none by Healy. He works his way methodically onward, avoiding the eyes of an orderly picking up laundry.

Only four more doors. What if Healy isn't here?

Room 706. One guy is at least eighty. His roommate is Chinese.

Come on . . .

704. At first glance, Gecko almost doesn't recognize Douglas Healy's unfeatures. His mane of sandy reddish hair is entirely concealed under thick bandages, and his face is pale gray, the pallor of death.

He's not dead, though. He's wearing an oxygen mask, there's an IV running into his arm, and a heart monitor measures his vital signs.

Dead people don't have vital signs.

Yet he's still deeply unconscious.

Gecko slips into the room, noting that the other bed is empty. Good. That makes it easier to sneak a peek at the chart that hangs on a clipboard at the footboard. Maybe that will supply a clue about when the patient might wake up and return home.

He never gets that far. The name on the folder

catches his attention and erases every other thought from his head.

Doe, John.

Healy's real name is Doe?

Then it hits him. John Doe is the name hospitals use for someone who can't be identified.

Healy had no wallet when we brought him in! They have no way to learn who he is!

He's startled by a soft voice from behind. "Do you know him?"

Gecko wheels. Standing there, bathed in sunlight from the window, is a slender blond-haired figure in a white lab coat.

A nurse?

No—he regards the girl in the doorway. Too young to be a nurse. She's around Gecko's age. His eyes travel to her badge: ROXANNE FITZNER, VOLUNTEER.

"Uh—no. I don't know him. I—uh—just—" For once, Gecko wishes he had the natural dishonesty of Terence, who can always come up with a lie to suit any situation.

Luckily, Roxanne feeds him the excuse he's looking for. "Are you with the school volunteer program? You know, you're not supposed to be on a patient floor without a badge."

"Right—uh—I wasn't sure where to check in."

She reaches into her pocket and produces an ID tag matching her own. "Bart Cranston wimped out, gutless wonder. He says he has a cold, but the truth is he doesn't want his lacrosse buddies calling him 'nursie.' The plastic opens up so you can write your name."

Gecko takes the tag and clips it to his shirt. "Thanks." He glances over at Healy. "What happened to this guy?"

Roxanne shakes her head sadly. "Mugged, probably. He was half naked when he turned up here. No wallet, no driver's license, deep concussion. They're not even sure he's ever going to wake up."

Gecko feels his core body temperature drop twenty degrees. Never wake up? So they're not murderers, but this is just as bad, maybe even worse!

Roxanne picks up on his agitation. "A word of advice," she says kindly. "Get a grip. None of these people are in the hospital because they feel great. If every sad case upsets you this much, maybe the volunteer gig isn't for you."

All Gecko can think of is escape. He can't stay here and look at the poor group leader for one more second—especially not when his distress is so obvious. If Roxanne can see it, any nurse or doctor might be able to put two and two together and realize that Gecko knows more than he's saying about the mystery patient.

"I—I gotta get back to school!" And he flees.

"Hey," she calls after him, "I didn't mean to scare you off."

But Gecko is already sailing past the nurses'

station for the exit. He ignores the elevators, opting for six flights of stairs—anything to put more distance between himself and what he, Arjay, and Terence have done.

The blocks back to school seem longer and even less friendly as he pounds down the street. Even in Atchison—a convicted criminal locked up with hundreds of the same—Gecko never felt that he himself was a bad person.

Until now.

He roars into English class just as the teacher is shutting the door.

"Nice of you to join us, Gecko."

"Sorry," Gecko rasps, collapsing into a chair.

He's never been sorrier.

Terence glares at the clock, trying to move the hands with the power of his mind. Never could he have imagined how long a class can last when you stick around for the whole thing. Years. Centuries.

He looks at his fellow students. These sheep, these mice, just sit there and take it. Of course, he's sitting right with them. There's a good reason for that. Hanging around stairwells and bathrooms would increase his chances of running into DeAndre, who he stood up last night. On top of everything else that went wrong, he left the kid with the razor-cut dollar sign standing on Second Avenue like he was waiting for a train.

True, there's an explanation. But not one he can give to DeAndre or anybody else. When someone has that kind of info, they've got power over you. You don't let that happen. Besides, a kid like DeAndre isn't interested in explanations. All he'll see is that he was dissed.

Not that Terence Florian is a wuss. But this is DeAndre's home turf, where he can call out his dogs. Around here, Terence's only dogs are Gecko and Arjay, and they're about as gangster as Dora the Explorer. *Vámanos.* What a waste. Arjay could be a crew all by himself. But despite his credentials, the big kid has no taste for street life.

The final bell is a hymn to freedom. Terence is the first one out the door, where a very powerful grip clamps on to his shoulder. Arjay, taking no chances, is waiting for him.

Terence is disgusted. "I said I was coming, didn't I? If I wanted to blow I would've done it last night."

"I trust you implicitly," the big boy tells him without a hint of irony.

Gecko is pacing just inside the main doors. Even from a distance they can tell that the ninth grader's face is green.

"I saw him."

"Healy?" Arjay demands.

Fighting back tears, Gecko brings them up to speed on his visit to the hospital. "They don't even know who he is. They've got him listed as John Doe."

Terence is thoughtful. "If they have no clue who they've got, then they also have no clue who's on the loose because of it."

Gecko bristles. "He might never wake up, and you don't even care!"

"I do so care," Terence defends himself. "But I also care that we don't get busted."

"The plan is still the same," Arjay decides. "We're in this with Healy. We have to believe he's going to come out of it."

Gecko takes the volunteer badge out of his pocket. "This gets me onto his floor to keep an eye on him. The minute he wakes up, we have to be there to apologize and set things straight."

Arjay takes a deep breath. "If we play our cards right, no one will even notice he's missing."

CHAPTER FOURTEEN

"Where's Doug?" asks Jerry, in the B.I.D. office above the Chinese restaurant.

Arjay struggles for nonchalance as he zips his coveralls. "Oh—running some errands."

Terence helps out by changing the subject. "Who's on garbage squad with us today?"

"A couple of the Sisters of Mercy went down to Atlantic City with the contents of the collection plate. Sweet gals, lousy blackjack players."

Terence drags himself downstairs with the others, and they join the nuns on the crowded avenue.

He sweeps up an apple core, nose wrinkling with distaste. Arjay and Gecko act so high and mighty. Like they're the only ones who feel bad about what's happened to Healy.

Do they think I'm such a rotten person that I'm happy the poor guy's lying like a carrot in a hospital bed?

Healy may be a jackass do-gooder, but nobody deserves that.

The events of the previous night come flooding back like a recurring bad dream. If those two had minded their own business, Healy never would have been on that fire escape in the first place.

And DeAndre and I would be splitting the take from those iPods. Savagely, he flicks a cigar butt down a sewer grating. *Time for a bathroom break. First of many.*

The restroom at Starbucks is empty. Too bad. A long line to get in kills even more time. As he opens the door, he's bumped from behind and catapulted inside. He bounces off the wall and recovers in time to see DeAndre flipping the lock.

Terence says the first thing that comes to his mind: "I can explain—"

But DeAndre is already reaching inside his jacket for his knife. Terence hurls himself onto the bigger boy's back, imprisoning the attacker's arms against his sides.

Undaunted, the razor-cut teen backs up and slams him against the hand dryer, which begins blowing loudly.

"Come on, man!" Terence shouts into the roar. "You're going to mess me up over a little mistake? There were *circumstances*!"

Wham! DeAndre drives him into the dryer again, and Terence sees stars. This time, the device falls off the wall.

"We'll do it again, man! Next time it'll be different!"

"You mean next time you're going to show up?" DeAndre snarls.

"You've got to understand," Terence pleads. "You know I'm on community service. There are people in my face! It's the price of doing business—it could be you one day."

Something about this makes sense to the razor-cut boy. The struggling subsides.

"Keep talking, yo."

Terence takes a chance and hops down, releasing his opponent. "I'll make it up to you. Next time, seventy-thirty split, your favor."

"How about a hundred-zero split?" DeAndre proposes darkly. "Here's how it's going to go down: you tell me the plan, and I hit the store with my crew. You get nothing. That's your penalty for last night."

Terence swallows a protest. Being cut out is bad enough. But when it's your own score, that's cold. It brings up some unpleasant memories from Chicago. Still, from the depths of his despair, he senses an opening.

"Okay. But then we're square. And from now on, I'm down with your crew."

DeAndre scowls. "Does your mouth ever stop working?"

Terence smiles endearingly. "What do you care, dog, so long as it's working for you?"

* * *

The new routine consists of trying to create the impression that the old routine is still in place. The boys follow their established schedule to the letter. They have one-sided conversations with the absent Healy to convince anyone who might be listening that they are still supervised. Mrs. Liebowitz never seems to notice that when they say, "Meet you downstairs, Mr. Healy," the group leader himself never appears.

"Dumb old bag never shuts up about how she's keeping an eye on us," is Terence's analysis. "Guess she should be keeping an eye on Healy."

Actually, their relationship with their neighbor from across the hall seems to be improving. At least Mrs. Liebowitz no longer fights with Arjay when he helps her carry her groceries up and her garbage down.

Gecko visits Healy at Yorkville Medical Center every chance he gets. The news is not good, but it isn't bad either. According to Roxanne Fitzner, the doctors say the coma doesn't appear to be deepening, and the brain activity is strong.

Roxanne seems to be at the hospital more than her home and school combined. "I'm a professional volunteer," she explains to Gecko. "My dad makes like, a gazillion dollars, and he gives absolutely nothing back to society. So I do everything I can to square up our family."

Gecko can't confirm her father's income, but he's never once been to the hospital without finding her there. She has an interest in Healy because she has an interest in every patient on the floor. Like Professor Belvedere, who lectured on high-level particle physics at Columbia but since his car accident doesn't remember what he had for breakfast thirty seconds before. Or Mrs. Gillespie, who feels fine except that she's become suddenly left-handed after getting a puck in the chin at a New York Rangers game.

One advantage of hanging out with Roxanne—Gecko is instantly established as a member of the school volunteer program. The nurses simply assume that any teenager with the blond girl is supposed to be there. His badge—which now reads Gecko Smith—opens the security doors, and he's got the run of the storage closet where the lab coats are kept. Not even in his own home has Gecko ever experienced such total acceptance. Too bad this can't be his community service instead of the B.I.D. It seems a lot more worthwhile than sweeping up candy wrappers on Second Avenue. Probably more fun too, except that when Gecko's at the hospital, he can't escape his crushing remorse over what's happened to Healy.

"You're a sensitive person," Roxanne says approvingly. "You really feel for these patients, especially John Doe. Just remember rule number one: get a grip. You can't let yourself become personally involved."

Too late for that. He's already personally involved in pushing the guy off a fire escape. As for her rule—Gecko hasn't had much of a grip on his life since Reuben first saw him behind the wheel of that go-kart.

For at least the twentieth time, he leans right into the group leader's pale face, looking for some sign of life and finds nothing.

"Come on, Mr. Healy," he whispers. "You've got to try harder!"

The electric guitar drops into Arjay's hands from the heavens.

Well, not really, but that's how it seems at first. He's in the school cafeteria, polishing off a truly disappointing tuna-salad sandwich, when the instrument is lowered into his arms.

Mr. Cantor, the music teacher, smiles down at him. "Come on, try it out."

Arjay plays a few experimental chords. He's not plugged in, of course, so he makes very little sound. But he's encouraged to find the frets exactly where they're supposed to be. The strings are looser than on his acoustic. He strums harder and faster. It's easy to see how rock guitarists slam out power chords. He replicates a Hendrix riff—badly—warbling the whammy bar.

"You're a natural," Mr. Cantor tells him.

Arjay grins at him. "I thought teachers were supposed to be honest."

"Never held an electric guitar in your life, not even jacked in, so you can't hear yourself—I'd say you're doing okay."

"It feels comfortable," Arjay admits, strumming the opening to "Ironman," which never sounds right on acoustic.

"A few weeks of practice, and you'll be the star of my stage band."

Arjay's smile disappears. "I told you—I can't."

"Your after-school job?" The teacher sits down beside him on the cafeteria bench, his expression kind. "Listen, Arjay. I did a little checking on you at the office. I know you've had problems with the law, and you're in some kind of group home. But if you'll let me talk to this Mr. Healy—"

Arjay sits forward in alarm. "You can't do that!"

"I've worked with kids like you before," Mr. Cantor assures him. "Trust me, getting you involved in normal, constructive activities is in everybody's interest here. He'll just have to tweak your schedule to get in an hour practice maybe two or three times a week—"

Arjay is adamant. "It's impossible!"

"He may seem overly strict to you, but when I explain—"

"You're not listening!" the big boy interrupts. "Promise you won't call!"

The music teacher looks bewildered, but he agrees. "All right."

Arjay stands up and hands back the guitar. "Thanks anyway."

Mr. Cantor makes no move to accept it. "How about this? We'll meet every day on your lunch hour. In the music room."

"I still can't be in your band," Arjay tells him.

"I'm a teacher. You're a kid with talent. I want to work with you." Mr. Cantor holds out his hand. "Rock and roll?"

The big boy shakes it. "Rock and roll."

When the trio walks into group therapy on Thursday afternoon, Gecko feels certain that Dr. Avery can read the guilt in their faces. But amazingly, the supermodel therapist picks up on nothing and focuses most of the hour on Casey Wagner, who has unveiled her newly revised top ten list of ways to die. (Space junk out, spontaneous human combustion in.)

Dr. Avery even compliments Gecko, Arjay, and Terence on their punctuality. The trio exchange knowing looks. It's Healy who was chronically late. The three of them are so paranoid about calling attention to their living arrangements that they follow every rule to the letter.

"That's where we're going to get busted," Terence warns. "Nobody is this good. It's unnatural, man."

It's true that the Alma K. Walker High School has never seen such conscientious students. Healy's unfixable bowling trophy, now duct-taped together, presides over some major homework battles. It's hard enough for Gecko and Arjay to get theirs done. Sitting on Terence and making him work sucks every ounce of energy out of them. It usually comes down to physical violence, and keeping a fight like that quiet takes even more energy than the fight itself.

A low profile is absolutely vital. Scrutiny—from neighbors, teachers, social workers, doctors, and even other teenagers—is the one thing they must avoid at all costs. No one can be allowed to reach the point where they decide to complain to Healy. There is no Healy.

"We were better off in jail," Terence moans from the depths of his algebra book. "At least nobody expects you to be smart. Think they're solving for *x* in lockup?"

Arjay is relentless. "We're not going back inside because you're too lazy to do what every other kid is doing right now."

"I'm not being lazy," Terence defends himself. "I'm just being *me*."

How can he ever explain it? Even when his old man used to threaten him with a copper pipe, nobody could make him study. They could force him physically into a classroom, but that was where the learning ended. To expect him to do this *now*, after a lifetime of slacking off, is like asking the guy who sweeps up in the missile silo to defuse a nuclear warhead. Right place, wrong person. It's not his gig.

The reading is pure misery. His teachers must all think he's got nothing better to do than sit around with his nose in some book! And to make matters worse, Jumbo stands over his shoulder, watching him do it.

"No wonder you hate this stuff, man!" the big boy exclaims. "You can barely read!"

His frustration with the work, and anger at Arjay for rubbing it in his face, is like nitric acid and glycerin sloshing around inside Terence. He wheels in his chair and starts throwing punches at his tormentor.

It takes Arjay and Gecko to pin him down. "I'm trying to help you!" Arjay pants, pressing Terence's shoulders into the carpet. "If you don't get better at reading, it's never going to stop being torture!"

"Listen to yourself, man," Terence mumbles resentfully. "You sound like a teacher. Don't you get it? Our jailer is gone, so now we're jailing ourselves. Even Healy wasn't as Nazi as you guys."

The whole world is upside down. With Healy in the hospital, the three finally have a chance to have some fun. Instead, they're waking up early, going to school and community service and therapy, and cleaning the apartment in case Ms. Vaughn pulls a surprise inspection.

That makes the least sense of all. "Listen, if that pickle-faced buster shows up here, we're all dead, no matter how clean the place is. You think she's going to say, 'Three felons are on the loose, but, hey, you could eat out of their toilet bowl, so no harm, no foul'?"

He listens raptly to Gecko's hospital reports, rooting for Healy to come home and get Arjay and Gecko off his back. But the group leader is still vegging, so the rat race goes on with no end in sight.

On Tuesday afternoon, they show up at the Business Improvement District to find the electronics store sealed off with yellow crime scene tape.

Never, not even when they shipped him from Chicago to that East Bumwipe Island, has Terence experienced such despair. Sure, he already knew DeAndre's crew would be taking the place down. But to actually see it—your plan working perfectly, with you on the outside—it feels like a death in the family.

On top of it all, Arjay gets suspicious when Terence spends the entire two-hour shift sweeping up around the yellow tape. "Tell me you don't know anything about this."

Terence turns furious eyes on him. "How could I know anything about anything? The only time I'm out of your sight is to go to the bathroom. Thanks for the privacy, by the way."

The next morning at school, DeAndre is waiting by the front entrance. His eyes never meet Terence's, and his lips never seem to move. But as he brushes by, he says very distinctly, "Got a present for yo." And he stuffs something into Terence's jacket.

Mystified, Terence inches a small flat item out of his pocket—a video iPod, brand new.

CHAPTER FIFTEEN

Gecko pushes the juice cart along the seventh floor hallway and stops to allow Roxanne to load up a tray of choices. She disappears into room 708, and he listens to her usual banter with the occupants.

"Hi, guys. Do you want the pheasant under glass or the beef Wellington? Oh, sorry. That's for the good patients. You two get cookies and juice. . . ."

Gecko smiles to himself. She's the ultimate volunteer, and everybody loves her. He looks forward to the weekend because it saves him the mad dash from school and back on his lunch hour. Plus he knows Roxanne basically lives here on Saturday and Sunday, so he'll be able to hang out with her. And he isn't exactly longing for apartment 4B either, where Arjay is "helping" Terence with his book report on *To Kill a Mockingbird*. The only thing more agonizing than making Terence read is making Terence write. Each letter is formed as if someone is holding a blowtorch to his wrist. By now, the two of them are probably rolling around on the living room floor, beating each other's head in.

Roxanne emerges. "Satisfied customers."

They work their way to the end of the hall, conspicuously skipping room 704, where Healy lies in comatose solitude, taking all his nourishment through a drip in his arm.

When they're done, Roxanne offers to take the cart back to the pantry. "Why don't you go sit with your John Doe," she suggests. "You've been eyeing that door all morning."

Room 704 is the place where the pleasant glow of the day turns chill. The patient's unmoving silence is such a stark contrast to the warm and vivacious atmosphere around Roxanne. It never fails to dampen his mood.

On Roxanne's advice, Gecko has been talking to Healy, praying that the sound of a human voice will percolate down to wherever his consciousness is hiding. "If nothing else, it'll make *you* feel better," is her philosophy.

And it does, kind of. It's a little less like he's visiting a corpse. "I got a B-plus on my chemistry report. The labs go a lot smoother now that Diego isn't so scared of me. All my grades are pretty good. . . ."

Funny he should be turning into a student now, of all times. It's almost as if school never really *counted* before. A bad grade was just a letter on a report card.

But these days, a blown quiz or ditched homework could set in motion a disastrous domino effect—a teacher slaps you with an F; Ms. Vaughn sees it on the weekly report; she calls Healy; he doesn't call back; she comes to the apartment to investigate. . . .

Fear is making me smarter.

Or maybe he always had the brainpower. Fear is just his motivation to use it.

". . . I'm doing better than I did in eighth grade, although that might have had a lot to do with my brother. He'd rip me out of bed at three a.m. and drag me off on some job. Next morning, I'd sleep through a test and take another zero. It gets to the point where you don't bother studying. . . ."

These conversations are obviously one-sided, so Gecko has to work in some natural pauses. He walks to the window and opens the blind. The slats of the venetians are dusty, and he rattles off four sharp sneezes in quick succession.

"Gesundheit."

He turns fast enough to pop all the disks in his neck. No doctor or orderly has entered the room. That's when he realizes that Douglas Healy is *watching* him.

Gecko's reaction is so electric that, in dashing over to Healy, he stubs his toe on the IV pole and very nearly winds up sprawled across the patient's bed.

"It's you! You're awake! We're so sorry! You *know* we didn't do it on purpose! We're okay! We're still in the apartment, doing all the things you set up for us, just praying that you'll get better and give us another chance!"

Healy's eyes are bloodshot and barely focused. "Do I know you?" The eyes widen. He's coming back, taking in his surroundings, working to dispel the fog. "What's your name?" Suddenly, his expression changes from confusion to alarm. "What's *my* name?"

Gecko is frozen to the spot.

"Gecko," comes a singsong voice, "it's time to take out the library cart." Roxanne pokes her head into 704. The shriek that escapes her is barely human. "Gecko, you did it! You reached him! You brought him back! Nurse! *Nurse!*"

Healy tries to lift himself up, but falls back, exhausted. "Get me a mirror! Please!"

Roxanne steps forward and flips open the rolling tray caddy.

John Doe stares at his reflection on the underside of the lid. "My God, I don't recognize my own face!"

It's plain from the panic in his voice that this is no mere groggy confusion. The patient may have been dazed at first, but he's wide-awake now.

The room fills with nurses and orderlies. Several interns come running, and finally a staff physician.

"I'm Doctor Radnor. Good to have you with us. What do you remember about what happened to you?"

Healy's voice is rising. "You're the doctor! You tell me! I don't even know who I am!"

"All right, calm down, sir. Let's take this one step at a time. . . ."

The room and everyone in it fade out for Gecko as his thoughts whirl. He alone knows Healy's true identity. The doctors should have it. *Healy* should have it.

But what would the result of that be? Gecko, Arjay, and Terence would be exposed, and Healy would be in no position to speak up for them. The halfway house would be closed, and its occupants issued a one-way ticket back into the juvenile justice system. All this with no assurance that the information would do anything to bring back the group leader's lost memory.

It's too much—too many twists and turns and surprises. Suddenly, Gecko can't stay in the room another second. He slinks out into the hall and collapses into a wheelchair parked by the wall.

He can't shake off the cold sweat that's making him weak and dizzy. There he sits, rocking slightly, hugging his shoulders and trembling. There's excited chaos in 704, but he hears only white noise.

Amnesia! After everything else that's happened, amnesia too. It's like all this is a bad movie, hatched from the twisted imagination of some sadistic screenwriter who specializes in worst-case scenarios.

Healy is the one person who has half a chance of

setting things right—but the guy in there isn't Healy anymore. And that's not even the worst part!

This is our fault. We took the only person who cared about us and ruined his life.

Surely there's nothing lower than that. This is absolute rock bottom.

A small hand appears on his hunched shoulder. He looks up to see Roxanne peering down at him, an intense expression on her face.

"I always figured it was just me," she murmurs huskily. "I hang around here, and it's more than a volunteer job. These patients are a part of my life. I thought I was the only one—until I met you. When I see you with John Doe—"

He shakes his head helplessly. "You were right—I have to get a grip."

In answer, she slides her hands behind his neck.

He almost smiles. "Not *that* kind of grip."

But she squeezes harder. Then his hands are on her arms, and he's squeezing too—the way a drowning man hangs on to a life preserver. The wheelchair begins to roll slowly backward as their faces draw closer, the two of them in a trance. She stumbles forward as the motion pulls him away from her. He holds on tight—not out of romance, but because human contact is the only thing that makes sense just then. In fact, it makes more sense than anything has in a long time.

When her lips meet his, it seems like the most natural thing in the world—to be kissing on a moving wheelchair in a hospital head trauma unit. It's a rush no Infiniti could match, not even one with a nuclear reactor under the hood.

There's a crash as the chair upends a rolling tray, sending clamps and scissors clattering to the floor.

Gecko and Roxanne stare at each other blearily, as if waking after a long sleep.

An orderly stands over the scattering of metal instruments. "Roxanne, could you give me a hand with this stuff?"

"Coming." Her eyes never leave Gecko.

He gets up from the wheelchair. "I should go."

She nods. "See you tomorrow?"

The simple question appears dizzyingly complex. The way events have been going lately, making plans twenty-four hours into the future seems like an insanely reckless thing to do.

He stammers, "Uh—right," because he wants it to be true. But that doesn't change the fact that he really needs to get out of there.

He sprints for the security door, shrugging out of his lab coat and tossing it into a laundry bin as he passes. Then down six flights of stairs, never pausing to catch his breath.

Roxanne! Talk about a bolt out of the blue. Of course he noticed her good looks before. But here at the hospital, he's got a lot more on his mind than hooking up—like devastating guilt and the terrifying uncertainty of the future.

Besides, who could have guessed that a totally hot girl would be into me?

The incredible fact that she *is* only mixes him up even more. A guy could get the bends from the highs and lows of this ride. The relief of Healy awake, the despair of his amnesia, Roxanne's lips—and now what? Home to tell Arjay and Terence their dilemma just got worse?

Gecko runs out of the building into the honking horns and other street sounds of the city. The chaos of New York seems simple and well ordered compared with the runaway train that is his life.

A UPS truck screeches to a halt beside him. The driver, obviously behind schedule, jumps down and races into the hospital carrying several small packages.

Gecko is in the van and behind the wheel faster than you could say *What can Brown do for you?* In that instant, he doesn't see a delivery truck, but a time machine. It can take him back before Healy, before Atchison, before the world got so complicated. Back to a day when all Gecko Fosse needed was a wheel in his hands and a motor roaring underneath him.

He shifts into drive and feels the transmission pull forward. His foot is half an inch from the pedal—he's visualizing himself wheeling into traffic—when it finds the brake again. He slams back into park and slumps in the seat.

No. That's the old Gecko, the one who could tell

himself he's just driving and ignore the fact that the car is filled with stolen goods and Reuben's gang of crooks.

Yes, things are crazy and getting crazier. But life has to be faced.

"Hey, you!" bawls a voice beside him. "Get out of there before I call a cop!"

Gecko steps down to the pavement. "There was a kid here who wanted to steal your truck," he tells the angry driver. "I chased him away."

CHAPTER SIXTEEN

Sometimes being totally screwed can set you free.

Strange but true, Arjay reflects as he walks down Lexington Avenue. When Gecko brought home the news that Healy's memory was gone, it seemed like the end of the world.

It was Terence who said, "Look at the bright side. When we thought he was coming back, we were slaves to that. Not anymore."

They're still going to school, and community service, and attending group therapy. The only difference is that it's no longer temporary.

Welcome to the new normal.

True, sooner or later, someone is going to check on them. The big question is when. It could be tomorrow; it could be months from now. As long as the school reports to Social Services stay positive; as long as there are no complaints from people like Jerry or Dr. Avery; as long as Ms. Vaughn's heavy caseload keeps her away from East Ninety-seventh Street, they just might be able to keep this going.

And as long as they stay afloat, there's a chance that something might save them. Arjay can't imagine what that could be. But it definitely won't happen if they're sitting in jail.

It reminds him of a story he studied in middle school. A condemned man staves off his execution by promising that, in a single year, he can teach the king's favorite horse to talk. Someone asks why he would make such a ridiculous bargain.

He replies, "A year is a long time. I may die. Or the king may die. Or the horse may die. Or the horse may talk."

Freedom equals possibility. The horse may talk.

Arjay has been locked up for so long, he barely remembers having a choice about what to do with his time. He has to get a life—literally. He walks with Gecko as far as Yorkville Medical Center, where the kid starts babbling about someone named Roxanne.

"Hold up." Arjay grabs him by the sleeve. "Who's Roxanne?"

Gecko hems and haws, but the embarrassed flush in his cheeks is as good as a lie detector test.

"You've been going to the hospital to keep an eye on Healy, and you wound up with a *girlfriend*?" Arjay demands.

"No!" Gecko defends himself. "At least, I don't think so. But you should see this girl, Arjay. You can't not like her. She's just a volunteer, but when she's on the ward, the whole place practically revolves around her. I mean, the seventh floor might as well just shut down if she ever stops going. . . ."

Arjay tunes him out. Well, that explains why Gecko hasn't been complaining about his countless jaunts to visit John Doe. A girlfriend! Even if it's an innocent crush, it's still dangerous. The more people who get to know them, the greater the chance that unwanted attention might fall upon their lives. In the scrutiny department, they can withstand exactly none.

He sighs. The increased risk is another part of their new reality. This isn't a couple-of-days kind of thing anymore. They can't stay locked in the apartment 24/7. God knows Terence isn't letting their situation cramp his style. He's already off on his own, looking for trouble. Arjay has no doubt he'll find it.

"Listen, Terence," Arjay told him, "I know what you consider a big night, and I'm not going to try to talk you out of it. *But be careful!* It's all our butts on the line, not just yours! And remember, if you get arrested, it means you read *To Kill a Mockingbird* for nothing!" He grins, recalling the look of horror on Terence's face.

He sends Gecko off with a similar warning, yet it's hard to be specific. Disaster is never far away, but the truth is they have no idea what to look for. It could be an inspection by Ms. Vaughn; it could begin as innocuously as this girl Roxanne saying "Let's go over to your house." Will Gecko have the brains to put her off? He's a fourteen-year-old kid. Who knows how smitten he is?

It's out of your control, Arjay reminds himself. Still, with memories of Remsenville permanently loaded in his cerebral hopper, it isn't easy to let the chips fall where they may.

He gets on the subway at Eighty-sixth street and rides downtown to Spring Street, where he heads east on foot. Nightlife begins to sprout around him. Snippets of live music escape from unmarked storefronts.

He's read about this area, but he never expected to have the freedom to experience it firsthand—not as a convicted felon in a halfway house.

A few more blocks and he's in the middle of it all. On the surface, it's a neighborhood of run-down tenements. Yet with the opening of every door, the pounding of drums, the thrum of bass, a few syllables of wailing vocals mingle in the street—a cacophonous mixture of rock, jazz, blues, funk, hip-hop, reggae, punk, and ska.

The club names are bizarre: Lucifer's Basement, Uber-freaky, Bottomless, This Ain't Kansas. After much deliberation, he selects the Green Zone, mostly because the words *no cover* have been acid-burned into the steel door. Zero is precisely the amount of money he has to invest in this expedition. Even with Social Services paying their rent and utilities, cash is becoming a problem. The hundred eighty bucks in Healy's wallet won't last long. Terence has managed to get his hands on another hundred by "unloading a couple pieces of consumer electronics." Arjay didn't ask for the details.

Inside the club, the air moves with the blast of sound that greets him. The bouncer thinks better of asking for ID—the newcomer doesn't seem very bounce-able. Arjay nods his thanks and pushes through a makeshift divider of hanging weather strips into the club proper, which is barely the size of the apartment on Ninety-seventh Street.

The band is called Collateral Damage—either slow punk or fast metal, and *very* loud. A mass of about forty die-hard fans are pressed to the claustrophobic stage, hopping with the beat, because horizontal movement is impractical. The only comfortable place to stand is at the back, by the bar, amid a late-teens/early-twenties assortment of piercings, tattoos, and black leather.

"Get you a beer, pal?" shouts the bartender over the roar of the music.

Arjay shakes his head no. He can't afford drinks; he's barely able to part with subway fare to get here. But the music is in the air, and poverty can't prevent him from listening.

Collateral Damage is pretty mediocre, yet Arjay inhales the experience, loving it as only a newbie can. He pays special attention to the guitarist, mentally translating the electric wail onstage to his ongoing lessons with Mr. Cantor. The relentless punk chords bear little resemblance to the music teacher's jazz/soft rock stylings, but he watches and learns, the fingers of his left hand running up and down imaginary frets. It's a night of wonder and discovery. As a caged animal in Remsenville, he forgot how it feels to *want* something. Why bother, when you have no chance of getting it?

I want to be that guy on the stage, I want to make music.

Collateral Damage finishes its set, relinquishing the stage to the next performers, Blecch Squad, and later, the headliners, Bad Haiku. Arjay basks in every decibel. Three bands in a shoe box club, one of dozens in the neighborhood, in a city of dozens of neighborhoods, one of dozens of cities where musicians hatch their strobe-lit dreams.

It's after three a.m. when the Green Zone finally disgorges its sweaty and exhausted slam dancers onto Chrystie Street. All the clubs have let out around then, and nobody wants to go home just yet.

Arjay loiters among the loiterers along a construction fence plastered with bills. There are ads for concerts, political rallies, independent films, and—what's this?

GUITARIST WANTED

ALL ORIGINAL MATERIAL/NO SKYNARD COVERS

HAIR-METAL WANNABES AND OTHER LAMERS
NEED NOT APPLY

At the bottom hangs a series of strips bearing the contact phone number. Most are pasted under by a flyer decrying the cultivation of broccoflower. But one still dangles free. Hand shaking, he tears it off and stuffs it in his pocket.

"Arjay?"

Only the lisp from her tongue stud gives her away. Casey Wagner blends into the downtown crowd so well that it takes a moment to recognize her. But come to think of it, this is exactly the place for her—with the spiked hair and punk clothes and attitude from the black lagoon. She fits right in. She probably reads out her death lists between sets.

"Oh, hi, Casey."

Her cheeks are flushed with excitement, which detracts somewhat from her complete lack of coloration. "Did you catch Drip Dry at the Puke Emporium? Man, they blew the roof off that dump!"

"I was at the Green Zone," he tells her. "Bad Haiku and a couple of other bands."

"You must have good ID. They're big-time gestapo over there. I can't believe it!"

"Nobody carded me."

"No, I mean I never would have pegged you as the type."

"What type?"

She shrugs. "You know—cool."

"Thanks," he says sarcastically.

"I love it down here," she enthuses. "It's so authentic."

"Authentic what?"

"You know, not plastic. When Zee Shrapnel choked on his own vomit, it was on *this corner*. Only—" She frowns. "Are you allowed to be out like this?"

Arjay bristles. "Are you?"

"My mom's sleeping pills are like nerve gas. I can come and go as I please. It's not the same with you. Didn't you, like, kill somebody?"

Most of the magic of the night evaporates with those words. "Listen, Casey. I'm breaking rules; you're breaking rules. Let's just leave it at that."

Leaving it at that is not Casey's strong suit. "But aren't you guys in some kind of halfway house thingie?"

Arjay sizes up the punk rock girl. She's probably harmless—good-looking even, if she'd lose some of the facial hardware. Yet there's nothing harmless about what would happen if word gets around that he, Gecko, and Terence are on their own, unsupervised in New York City. A curfew violation is a minor infraction, but if it invites inspection, they might as well be caught robbing banks and garroting puppies.

The old wartime warning jumps to mind: *Loose Lips Sink Ships*. What lips could be looser than a pair pierced by half a dozen metal rings?

He has to close this subject permanently.

"No offense," he says carefully. "I've got two other guys in this with me. I can't talk about it."

"It'll be our secret," she says with a conspiratorial smile.

Arjay swallows hard. The last thing he wants is to share a secret with Casey, who sees Dr. Avery, who, in turn, reports to Ms. Vaughn. But what choice does he have?

They shake on it.

CHAPTER SEVENTEEN

For John Doe, the world has become a strange and uncomfortable place.

How could it be otherwise? A grown man—between thirty-five and forty, the doctors estimate—waking up in a hospital bed with no idea who he is or what's happened to him.

Concussion, they say. That's not hard to believe. The former Douglas Healy feels like someone has taken a baseball bat to his head. And anyway, the diagnosis is right there on the chart. *Acute retrograde amnesia resulting from blunt force trauma to the upper cranial region.*

"In other words, you bonked your conk," Dr. Radnor explains. "Incidentally, the fact that you can read your chart is important. In total amnesia, a patient might forget the English language. He might have to relearn how to reach up and scratch his nose when it itches. This proves you have *some* memory."

"What good is that if I don't even know my own name?"

"Don't rush yourself," the doctor advises. "You know you're a human being. You know you're an American. You know you're in New York City—"

Healy is agitated. "Because you told me!"

"But you know what New York City *is*. Your mind hasn't been wiped clean. You were in a coma for more than a week. That's not a small thing. But I have every confidence that a good portion of your memory will return. You just have to be patient."

That's easy for Radnor to say. He isn't the one who's been plunked in the middle of a world that's a complete mystery. It's like walking into a movie halfway through, not recognizing the plot or any of the characters. Only that movie is your *life*.

He tries to reason through his predicament, but that leads him down even more upsetting lines of inquiry. For example, does he have a wife and family somewhere, devastated, wondering where he is?

Turns out, the police have already thought of that. "We've been combing missing person reports," Detective Sergeant DaSilva informs him. "So far no luck."

"What does that mean?" Healy demands. "Nobody's looking for me?"

"Not necessarily. The world's a big place. Lots of different databases to check. Or maybe you just haven't been reported AWOL yet."

"How could that be? I've been in this hospital for days."

"Maybe you're the kind of guy who likes to disappear for a while—the lost weekend type," the cop suggests. "Or you could have been on a business trip when you got hurt. Happens all the time. Nobody misses you because they know you're out of town."

The sergeant's all-business attitude only raises Healy's level of agitation. "How can you be so calm about this? I could be anybody! What if I'm a criminal?"

DaSilva shrugs. "Then I'll arrest you. But I doubt that's it. Most of our lives aren't that dramatic."

Says who? For John Doe, it's all drama, all the time. What if he has no health insurance? Does he have a bank account? A home? In New York or in Timbuktu? How will he know where to go when he's discharged? What will he wear? These borrowed hospital scrubs are his only clothes. The emergency room staff threw out the bloodstained T-shirt and gym shorts they found him in.

When that pretty volunteer, Roxanne, asks how he takes his coffee, he can only stare at her blankly. He has no idea. For all he can remember, he might not even drink coffee.

Roxanne favors him with a dazzling smile as she fills his cup. "In that case, you're our dream customer. You can't say the coffee's bad if you don't know what it tastes like when it's good."

She's a great kid, but all the forced cheeriness is starting to get on Healy's nerves. Smiles from the doctors, the nurses, the orderlies, the volunteers. It's one thing to stay positive, but it's a little insulting to his intelligence. His life, whatever it was, is in shreds. Grinning isn't going to change that.

The boy who calls himself Gecko leans over and whispers, "Try it black with one Sweet'n Low."

Healy frowns. "What, you've got psychic powers?"

Gecko can be a bit of an oddball—friendly one minute, quiet and withdrawn the next, like he's hiding a deep dark secret. "Something like that," he mumbles evasively.

The kid has at least one thing going for him: Roxanne. They don't seem to be officially dating, but no one can miss the way they look at each other.

Not that the patient is minding their business. Still, when your entire life has been erased in the blink of an eye, on top of all your other problems, you're bored out of your mind. You need something to think about. Around this place, the only entertainment is the soap opera of Gecko and Roxanne. He throws out a few feelers, but all the two teenagers will cop to is what great friends they are, and how much they respect each other's volunteer work. True, they could be hiding something. Then again, maybe sweet kids like that are just too shy to make a move.

"Well, when I was your age," Healy tells Gecko

meaningfully, "I would have been madly in love with her."

His brow clouds. The truth is, John Doe has absolutely no idea what he was like at Gecko's age or any other. For all he can tell, he was disgorged from the Great Space Ark and teleported to earth, his mind a blank slate.

Gecko Fosse is on the couch in the staff lounge of Yorktown Medical Center, making out with Roxanne and not thinking. The not thinking part is crucial. He's not thinking about the fact that Healy's memory shows no sign of returning. He's not thinking about the fact that his entire life sits on a foundation that doesn't exist. And he's especially not thinking about the fact that the blame for all this lies with him—and Arjay and Terence.

Just as he was able to edit "getaway" from "driver" when he was behind the wheel, he can separate his first experience of having a girlfriend from the disastrous events that made it possible. A few closed doors away, poor Healy is being wheeled in for yet another ultrasound, CT scan, or MRI. But all it takes is one taste of the strawberry flavor of Roxanne's lip gloss, and he's lost in the strange yet wonderful world of the two of them.

"Get a grip," she murmurs into his lips.

"*You* get a grip."

"No—*you*."

"You!"

A grip on reality is impossible for Gecko, so he substitutes a physical grip on Roxanne. It works okay, so long as you're good at not thinking.

Their relationship takes place entirely inside Yorkville Medical Center. Their moments together have to be stolen between the dozens of tasks the overworked nurses always seem to find for them. Gecko is amazed at Roxanne's uncanny ability to come up with recreational uses for the ordinary things found in a hospital ward. Leaky IV bags, no longer usable, make excellent squirt guns; two wheelchairs in a secluded hallway virtually beg to be drag raced. She lets him into her secret game of nicknaming each patient after a historical figure. The man in 740 becomes Julius Caesar because his narrow fringe of hair resembles a laurel wreath. Nostradamus can always predict what kind of cookies will come with the tea cart. There are General Patton, Elvis, Mother Teresa, Peter the Great—the list goes on.

The one patient who is immune to all this is Healy. Roxanne catches on quickly that, for Gecko, John Doe is untouchable. There is something different about the way Gecko views the occupant of room 704, and her instincts tell her that she shouldn't even ask about it.

Gecko knows that he'll never "get a grip" on what's happened to Douglas Healy. And no amount of strawberry lip gloss is ever going to change that.

* * *

Arjay squeezes the tube, carefully tracing a bead of caulk around the lip of the basin.

Mrs. Liebowitz peers over his shoulder. "When did you learn all this?"

The big boy shrugs. There are classes in juvie, but in adult prison, they teach you a trade. "You'll have to use the bathroom sink for a day or so to give the silicone a chance to cure."

Terence sticks his head into apartment 4A. "Telephone, dog. Guy says his name is Rat Somebody."

Arjay caps the tube. "It won't leak anymore, ma'am."

Mrs. Liebowitz frowns at him. "Arjay—"

He stops at her door.

"How's Mr. Healy making out with the three of you? I—" She hesitates. "I haven't seen him around much."

He swallows hard. "Social Services has him buried in paperwork. Just knock if you have any more problems with the sink." He runs across the hall to 4B.

"You Arjay?" asks the voice on the phone.

"That's me." The guitarist ad! Who else would call this number and ask specifically for him?

"What are you, like, twelve?"

"I'm nineteen," he lies. He may sound young, but at six foot five, he'll have little trouble passing for older in person.

"Be here in twenty minutes. Five forty-one East Sixth."

Arjay scribbles it down on the back of an envelope. "What apartment?"

"You'll know." *Click.*

When Mrs. Liebowitz looks out her window a few minutes later, she sees Arjay in full flight down Ninety-seventh Street, his guitar slung over his hulking shoulders.

Raw punk blares from the open windows, filling the street as if the row house is a three-story speaker. No wonder the caller didn't bother to provide an apartment number. Find the source and you've found the band.

As Arjay climbs the broken stairs, the physical effect of the music on his body increases. The drumbeats are concussion bombs, the guitar chords a stomach-churning buzz. The thrum of the bass can be felt below the gum line. It's even better than the Green Zone. Anyone can go to a show. This is *inside*.

The door is missing. In its place hangs a large grease-stained New York Rangers jersey, cinched curtain-style with electrical tape. Arjay pushes through for his first glimpse of the band. They stop playing at the sight of him, generating a pulse of sudden quiet that nearly knocks him over.

The three young men are pale and death-camp skinny. I probably outweigh the whole group! he thinks. With the drum kit thrown in for good measure.

The singer scowls at Arjay's guitar. "What the hell is *that*?"

"It's what I learned on. In jail." He has a sense that his stint in Remsenville, the greatest tragedy of his life, might somehow enhance his credibility with the skeptical band members.

The singer shrugs out of his electric and offers it to Arjay.

His fingers move experimentally over the frets. To his great relief, everything feels familiar to the school guitars he's been practicing on with Mr. Cantor. He strums an air chord.

"Helps if you make contact," the bassist offers.

He plucks a high E and is startled that the resulting note comes not from the instrument itself, but from the speakers. It bears little resemblance to the cheap, tinny amplifiers in the Walker music room. He tries a C chord and is rewarded by an authoritative blast, louder than he expected, distorted and powerful.

It sounds like rock and roll.

He can't help grinning. "It's great."

The singer is losing patience. "We don't give lessons. Can you play?"

"I can play."

And now he believes it.

CHAPTER EIGHTEEN

One thirty a.m. Terence time.

The streets are quiet, but the avenues are still lively. New York City is all about choice. It's your call whether or not you want to be in the middle of the action.

Tonight, Terence has a specific destination in mind—a high-rise apartment building on East One-hundred-and-fifth Street, close to the river.

He's scoped the place out in daylight. Big—thirty stories, maybe thirty-five. Not the projects exactly, but definitely not the high-rent district. And as he suspected, dark and deserted at half past one in the morning.

Keeping to the shadows, he searches for the spot he scouted before. Jackpot. A row of quarter-circular iron bars block access to a narrow, street-level basement window. At some point, a car or truck must have backed into this protective cage. Three of the pieces have been torn free of the brick.

Terence pulls a crowbar from under his jacket and goes to work, prying the iron arches away from the wall. Then he smashes the glass and squeezes feetfirst through the window frame, dropping to the concrete floor.

It's a laundry room, smelling faintly of motor oil, detergent, and lint. He navigates the maze of idle washers and dryers, smirking through an obstacle course of very large women's underwear strewn on the cement. Finally, he's in the main hallway. He passes the furnace, several storage closets, and a reeking trash compacter. At last, a heavy metal door. He tries the handle. Locked.

No problem. From his pocket he produces a small plastic card—Douglas Healy's library card, to be precise—and deftly inserts it into the frame by the knob. There is a click, and the door swings wide. The elevator is directly in front of him.

Cake.

He rides to the twenty-seventh floor and follows the corridor, his sneakers barely touching the carpet. The Ninja Walk. That's what his dogs back in Chicago called it. They had to give him props for that, even if they never appreciated anything else he had to offer. Soundless movement, like the wind.

Apartment 27B is locked with a dead bolt. No problem. He takes out a flathead screwdriver and a thin piece from a nutcracker set. Good picks, nutcrackers. Only dental instruments make better burglar tools. He's inside in three minutes.

The apartment is a disappointment. It's *nice*. Terence was expecting something a little more *Boyz in the Hood*. Oh well, doesn't matter. This isn't about the crib. He's here to make a statement.

He advances cautiously, unfolding a small piece of paper from his pocket. Now to find the right bedroom . . .

The lights flash on, and he wheels to see varnished wood and the Louisville Slugger logo speeding toward him. In a burst of survival instinct, he ducks and feels a breeze as the home run swing passes half an inch over his head.

A middle-aged woman wrapped in a voluminous flowered nightgown has him cornered in the hallway.

"You picked the wrong house to rob, little man!" she seethes, her eyes wide and bulging. "You want my diamond necklace? My ruby slippers?"

"It's not like that—" Terence tries to explain.

"Why? Because I'm the one holding the bat?" The woman shoulders the Slugger for another cut, and that's when Terence makes his move. He springs forward and somersaults under the swing, rolling up onto his feet behind her.

He's reaching for the knob and a highlight-film escape when the door is thrown open, and he collides with a familiar razor-cut.

"You!" DeAndre exclaims in shock.

"Call her off, man, she's going to kill me!" Terence croaks.

"Call *who* off?"

"The crazy lady!"

The sight of Terence and DeAndre together draws a gasp of horror from the woman's lips. "You hurt my boy, and I'll splatter you all over that wall!"

"Nobody's getting hurt, Mama," DeAndre says. "I know this yo."

She lowers the bat, but only slightly. "DeAndre Rhodes, how many times have I warned you about the jailhouse trash you call friends? Fine people who break into houses at—" She stares at the kitchen clock. "Where do you get off rolling home at two o'clock in the morning? As long as you live under my roof—"

"I got *busy*, Mama." DeAndre snatches the paper from Terence's hands and peers at the note.

> Impressed? You should be.
> Terence

DeAndre is disgusted. "I hope *you* know what you're talking about, yo, 'cause I must be missing something."

Terence shuffles uncomfortably. "Mind taking this outside?" He gestures meaningfully in the direction of DeAndre's mother.

She shakes the Slugger threateningly. "Don't you

act like I'm a blind woman, DeAndre! I got no respect for the life you've been leading! I can use this bat on you too!"

Her son ushers Terence into the hall. "Get some sleep, Mama," he tosses mildly over his shoulder. "Remember your blood pressure." He turns murderous eyes on Terence. "I could carve you up like roast beef! What jury's going to convict me after you threatened my mama?"

"More like your mama threatened me," Terence mumbles.

"That why you came here? To play Bad Boys of Comedy?"

"To make a point!" Terence counters. "Look how easy I got into your crib. You could be waking up tomorrow with this note on your pillow!"

"So?"

"So I got talent! You *need* me, you and your crew. That last score—pretty sweet, right? Plenty more where that came from."

The snake eyes narrow. "You got something in mind, or are you just talking out of your butt, as usual?"

Terence grins.

CHAPTER NINETEEN

John Doe's head wound heals. The mummylike dressing on his crown is replaced by a simple gauze bandage. There's no unsteadiness or hesitation to his movements. He feels good. There's only one problem: his memory is still missing in action.

Dr. Radnor puts Roxanne and Gecko in charge of showing the patient flash cards with pictures of common objects. Healy has no trouble recognizing a pickup truck, a cell phone, or a banana, but his own name continues to elude him.

"I know what things are called," he explains mournfully. "I haven't lost the world; it's myself I can't remember."

"You shouldn't rush it," is the doctor's opinion. "It may not be overnight, but your past *will* return to you. Retrograde amnesia is rarely permanent."

It's little consolation to Healy, and also to Gecko, who feels the group leader's plight pressing relentlessly on his conscience.

Twenty times a day he has to hold himself back from bursting out with *Your name is Douglas Healy!* Who knows—maybe those five words will jump-start the poor man's brain.

But he can't do it. Not until Healy is in a position to stick up for them with Ms. Vaughn.

He moved heaven and earth to give us a second chance. We have to assume he wants us to stay out of jail.

They have no choice but to wait for his memory to come back on its own.

The homework wars have subsided somewhat, mostly because Arjay now spends every spare minute practicing. He's got nine days to learn the entire repertoire of "This Page Cannot Be Displayed," a ska-influenced punk combo "too indie for the independents, too down for downtown, too loud to exist." At least, that's what it says on the posters advertising This Page's first gig of the Arjay Moran era, scheduled for a week from Saturday at a club called Pus Groove.

He listens to the songs on headphones, his fingers dancing across the frets of the electric Fender. Everything is borrowed—Rat Boy's demo disk, Voodoo's CD player, and a school guitar, only slightly broken, courtesy of Mr. Cantor. Rat Boy is the singer and front man, with Voodoo on drums. (The final This Page member, the bassist, has no name—it's the next new thing, he believes—though it still says Scott Kroshinsky on his driver's license.)

"You guys need a new name," Terence's opines. "How about Brown Day?"

Arjay is annoyed. "You can't even hear it!"

Gecko looks up from Healy's laptop computer, where he's typing the group leader's weekly report to the Department of Social Services. "I can hear it. It's pretty loud."

"I'm trying to read, here," Terence complains. "Doing homework because the last time I tried to kick back, the big dog damn near strangled me." He holds up his copy of *Wiseguy*.

"From *To Kill a Mockingbird* to a mob book," Gecko says sarcastically. "You're a regular professor."

"Shows what you know," Terence sneers. "*This* is real life—making scores, outsmarting the cops, putting together a crew. No mockingbirds—is that even a real bird?"

"That explains the D minus," Gecko shoots back.

"How about a little respect?" Terence peers over his shoulder at the laptop. "Typical—you got Jumbo doing odd jobs for people around the building, and you're getting great grades. What about me?"

"What *about* you?"

"I should have some accomplishments too."

"You said you don't care what a bunch of suits think of you," Gecko reminds him.

"Am I your dog or what? Put that I got voted school president."

Arjay lifts the headphones off his ears. "No way—

nothing the dragon lady can check on."

"Something else, then," Terence persists. "Show me a little love. I'm the one bringing in all the cash."

"All the cash?" Gecko repeats. "A hundred bucks—that goes pretty fast when you're feeding three people. We're going to have to find a way to make some money. You know what dinner is tonight? Mustard sandwiches."

"So buy food!"

"And pay for it with what?" Gecko challenges. "Healy's stash is almost gone. If we can't make it last, juvie's going to be the least of our worries."

"I should have a little money after the show on Saturday," Arjay puts in. "It won't be a ton, but the band gets a cut of the gate."

"If they give you what you deserve, we'll be broke from funeral expenses," Terence announces.

"At least he's *contributing*!" Gecko exclaims.

"I've got something in the works," Terence says haughtily. "Pretty soon we'll have more green than we know what to do with."

Arjay is wary. "I hope it's got nothing to do with that kid with the dollar sign on his head. That's a gang member if I ever saw one."

"What do you know about it?" Terence snaps. "That's how it *works*. You get down with a crew. You look out for them; they look out for you. That's how it was in Chicago; that's how it is here."

"Just be *careful*," Arjay insists. "If you screw up, we take the fall with you."

Terence kicks the TV cart, causing the duct-taped figure to fall off the bowling trophy for the umpteenth time. "*I'm* the one who has to be careful? You joined a *band*, man! Lover boy's got a girlfriend!"

"She knows nothing about us," Gecko defends himself. "She thinks I'm in the volunteer program, like her. She doesn't even go to our school; she's in some private academy. I think her family has money."

"Chicks are nosy, man," Terence lectures. "The longer you're together, the more she's going to start snooping around your life. Don't tell her anything stupid—like the truth."

Gecko doesn't admit it, but Terence's prediction has already begun to come true. A lot of his precious time with Roxanne is spent steering the conversation away from subjects like "your apartment," "your friends," and "your family."

He provides as little information as possible. "I have an older brother. I haven't seen him in a few months."

It's not easy to keep secrets from Roxanne. Her interest in others is so genuine that it's impossible to put her off. "Is he away at college?"

"Right, upstate." Attica.

As he avoids the subject of family with Roxanne, he realizes he's been doing the same with himself for years. It's the not thinking all over again. Spending his childhood in Reuben's getaway-driver boot camp, with Mom either absent, exhausted, or both, never seemed abnormal to Gecko. It was the only life he knew.

Look at Arjay. Every day is a personal battle to keep himself from picking up the phone and calling his parents.

Why don't I feel like that?

The Fitzners are wealthy, but Gecko isn't jealous of their money. The source of his envy is this: when Roxanne talks about family, it's clear that she's one hundred percent comfortable in her sense of belonging.

I never felt like that with Reuben and Mom. Not for a month; not for an hour.

It only rubs it in when she makes the assumption that his family must be similar to hers. "Your folks must be proud of your brother. My sister Dori was supposed to go to college, but at the last minute, she decided to travel around the world instead. My dad is hopping mad. He made this big donation to Yale, only to have her split for the airport with her boyfriend. He thinks all men are trying to lead his little girls astray. I can't wait till he meets you."

Gecko nearly rolls off his chair. "Meets me?"

"You're so different," she explains. "Daddy's been on Wall Street too long. He thinks everybody's got some kind of hidden agenda. But you're so honest and genuine. I think you might short-circuit his whole belief system."

"No, what I mean is—" He swallows hard. "Uh—*how* would he meet me?"

"My parents are having a party on Sunday." She reads the reluctance in his eyes. "You *have* to come! It'll be so boring without you! I'll be trapped on my dad's boat. I'll go nuts. Please say yes!"

Not much has made sense lately, but Gecko is certain of this: stranding himself on a floating interrogation room to be subjected to the prying questions of countless strangers has got to be one of the stupider options for a Sunday afternoon.

"Sure, Rox. I'll be there."

The smile on her face makes it all worth it.

Sunday is cool but clear. Brilliant sun glitters off the chrome fittings on the watercraft that ring the small harbor. A dozen boats fill the rectangular inlet at the World Financial Center.

Gecko has no idea where to meet Roxanne. He's already late, thanks to a subway breakdown at Twenty-third Street.

Then he spots her. She's with several uniformed crew members who are escorting well-dressed ladies and gentlemen up a red-carpeted gangway to a massive high-tech yacht.

He gapes. *This* is "my dad's boat"? The ship is moored alongside the dock because lengthwise it wouldn't fit in the harbor. The gleaming superstructure towers over everything else in the inlet. A small bubble helicopter peers down from its space atop the helipad.

She notices him and waves. "Gecko!"

He's rooted to the spot. Even a kid who comes from nothing can tell the difference between rich and superrich.

Eventually she comes over to get him. "Get a grip," she murmurs and kisses him.

"I'm working on it," he tells her. In reality, the only grip he's getting is on just how loaded the Fitzners have to be.

She takes him by the arm and introduces him to the crew. He shakes several white-gloved hands. Every single sailor shoots him a protective, vaguely threatening glance. They seem to love Roxanne just as much as the patients and staff at the hospital do.

"Good to meet you," Gecko stammers, feeling like a low-class dope who has never seen a yacht before, and never will again.

They walk up the gangway and step onto the varnished deck. The watercraft is a floating version of one of those fancy Las Vegas hotels on TV. Everything is shiny chrome, polished and perfect.

Roxanne interprets his awe as reluctance. "It won't be so bad. Once you've met my parents' boring friends, we're totally off the hook. There are a lot of good places to disappear on this crate."

Gecko can believe it. "You know, Rox, when you talked about your dad's boat, I thought it was, you know, a *boat*."

She nods her understanding. "That's Daddy for you. He loves Mom too much to trade her in for a trophy wife, so he went all *Lifestyles of the Rich and Famous*. Only he works so hard to pay for this stuff that he has no time to enjoy it. Come on, let's see if the helipad's open. Great views of the Statue of Liberty."

They sit side by side on the pad, leaning on the chopper and each other, as the yacht slips out of the boat basin and takes to the gentle waves of the Upper Bay. Gecko has been living in New York for more than a month, yet he's never seen the famous skyline from a distance before. The moment is so perfect it's almost painful—Roxanne on his arm, the entire city stretched out in front of them.

She burrows her face into the skin of his neck. "I used to ride up here with my mouth wide open," she murmurs. "I told my parents I was eating the wind."

A sailor pokes his head through the access hatch. "Got her," he says into his walkie-talkie. "Roxie, how many times do we have to tell you the helipad's off-limits?"

"I like the view," she shoots back cheerfully.

"Well, take one last look, because you're coming down. Your father suggests that you mingle with the guests."

"*Suggests?*" she returns. "He stopped barking orders long enough to suggest something?"

"And he wants to meet your friend," adds the crewman. "Let's go."

Gecko swallows hard.

As they descend the companionway, Roxanne squeezes his hand. "Don't look so terrified," she whispers. "He's going to love you."

After all the buildup, the famous Mr. August Fitzner turns out to be a slightly pudgy middle-aged man in a blue blazer and white slacks.

"Gecko," the multimillionaire repeats thoughtfully. "Is that Estonian?"

His daughter grins. "It's lizard, Daddy."

Gecko blushes. "It's a nickname. My real name is Graham."

"Nicknames are for the young," announces one of Mr. Fitzner's companions. "I went by Curly in my police academy days. What I wouldn't give for somebody to call me that now." He pats his bald head.

Everyone laughs politely except Gecko, who has heard the magic word: *police*.

"If you ever watch the news, Gecko, you'll probably recognize Deputy Chief Mike Delancey."

And there's the convicted felon, the fugitive from a defunct halfway house, shaking hands with the number two cop in New York City.

Arjay would have a heart attack.

CHAPTER TWENTY

The cover charge at Pus Groove is ten dollars, but that means nothing to Terence. He merely points to the group that has just been admitted and says, "They paid for me." Just like that, he's in, melting into the noisy crowd. This place is far too packed and too loud for the bouncers to figure out who belongs and who doesn't.

Besides, paying is for suckers. A baboon could get in free. Well, maybe not. Because there's Gecko being carded and turned away.

It figures. Terence wouldn't be caught dead in this headbanger heaven, full of stooges from the suburbs who think this is "the edge." It's Gecko who's convinced him they have to be there to support Arjay at his first gig. And the dumb kid can't even get past the gate.

I should just take off. Like Jumbo cares if I come to his show or not.

With a sigh of resignation, he pushes his way to the emergency exit and opens the heavy door. No alarm sounds. He's not surprised. Pus Groove is so dilapidated it's amazing the roof stays on.

"Gecko!" he hisses. "Get in here!"

The fourteen-year-old slinks down the alley, and Terence hustles him inside.

"Real smooth, man!" Terence says sarcastically.

Gecko is defensive. "What can *I* do if the guy cards me?"

Terence regards him pityingly. "He carded you because you stood there with your stupid puppy eyes saying, 'please let me in.' You've got to show some attitude." No wonder Gecko worships Douglas Healy. The kid is a newborn. He couldn't have lasted much longer in juvie.

As they descend the tunnel-like staircase, the roar of the music swells. Terence winces in true pain. He's got nothing against volume, but in this case that's all there is. Haven't these idiots ever heard of hip-hop?

"I hope Arjay's band is better than this!" Gecko shouts in his ear.

Fat chance.

Downstairs is a crush of dancing, gyrating people who don't seem to notice how pathetic the music is, or don't care.

The Keelhaulers clatter to a merciful end, and there's blessed quiet for a few seconds until a deejay puts on something even worse.

Terence takes advantage of the migration toward the bar and bathroom to grab Gecko and worm their way up front. No point in supporting Arjay if Arjay can't see them there, supporting him.

All at once, Gecko is pulling on his sleeve.

"Cut it out, man! You trying to get us bounced?"

"Terence—look!"

It's Casey Wagner, the doom-crier from their therapy group. He's surprised to see her at first, but on second thought it makes sense. This is her kind of place—her music, and her crowd, her Disney World version of living dangerously.

"We can't let her see us!" Gecko hisses. "If she mentions it at group, Avery might try to get in touch with Healy—and you know where that leads!"

Terence regards him in amusement. "Fine, we'll lay low. But how's she supposed to overlook that two-hundred-sixty-pound clodhopper when Brown Day hits the spotlight?"

"We could go backstage and warn him!" Gecko persists. "Maybe he'll call off the show!"

Terence snorts. He's not as freaked as the others about being exposed. When it all falls apart, he intends to run away. It's not rocket science. "Lighten up, Gecko. This is the guy's dream—to play bad music in a toilet. Whatever happens, happens."

If Gecko wants to argue, he's too late. First the lights are cut, plunging the club into darkness. Next a guitar chord sounds so loud, so raw, that Terence can feel his cuticles shrinking back into his fingers. Then the lights blaze on, and the onslaught of This Page Cannot Be Displayed is unleashed on the patrons of Pus Groove.

Terence isn't a fan of this kind of music, but he can tell from the reaction of the audience around him that This Page is making a big impression. From the very first note, the crowd has come alive, bouncing like pogo-stickers minus the hardware.

Rat Boy, the singer, is darting around the stage like a bat with faulty sonar. Voodoo is just a blur at the drums. The no-name bassist is kicking like a chorus girl while delivering background chords like depth charges.

But all eyes are on Arjay Moran. He's just standing there, really, not strutting like the others, barely moving. But the sheer size of him, and his intense concentration—it's obvious that his presence and sound are something new and special. It's impressive, and Terence doesn't impress easily.

Over the assault of pure punk, he can hear the words "new guitarist" shouted from mouth to mouth.

"Who *is* that?"

"Wasn't he with E Coli before this?"

"Naw, that guy was half the size of him!"

"Maybe he's from the West Coast!"

"Forget the West Coast!" Terence bellows into the fray of speculation. "I'll tell you who that is—*that's my dog*!"

As the show goes on, Arjay's performance becomes more daring, more creative, and more spectacular. By the time Rat Boy introduces the band, the guitarist he calls Arjay receives an ovation that literally brings the house down. Plaster drifts from the ceiling as roaring fans stamp the floor and pound the walls.

The set goes on longer than expected because there are four encores. There'd be more, but This Page has run out of material. The stage is doused with airborne drinks as the band departs—the ultimate tribute.

One amplifier short-circuits in a shower of beer and sparks. There's a delay before the next band can come on. The deejay fills the silence with more ghastly noise.

Gecko is glowing with excitement as he wheels on Terence. "He's really good!"

Terence nods grudgingly. "If he played decent music, he could be a star. Let's go backstage and say hey."

A few seconds later, struggling to make progress through the sea of fans, they find themselves face-to-face with Casey.

"Omigod, you guys! Why didn't you tell me?"

Terence tries to play it down. "It's no biggie, girl. Everybody's got a hobby."

"Are you kidding me? I'm down here every weekend—*all* these people are! We have a good time, but you know what *really* keeps us coming back? The thought that one day maybe we're going to hear something different! Something revolutionary! An *artist*! I can't believe he's on parole!"

Gecko bristles. "He's not on parole!" Technically, the three of them are still in custody. Parole is something they can only dream about.

"I mean whatever you guys are on. They must ride you pretty hard. And instead of just surviving, Arjay finds a way to develop a great talent. How does he do it?"

"He's got it going on," Terence acknowledges with a yawn.

"No, I mean how does he *actually* do it?" Casey persists. "I want to talk to him, find out about his creative process."

"We'll let him know you're looking for him," Terence drawls, accidentally on purpose allowing the flow of bodies to separate them.

The tiny backstage area doubles as an office and storage locker. It's bedlam, with This Page fresh from their set, and the headliners, who are waiting for the sizzling amp to be replaced so they can go on.

A slick-haired thirtysomething in a black turtleneck is schmoozing Arjay and his band-mates.

"It's never too early to think about hooking up with a good manager. If we can get you seen by the right people, a recording contract is a slam dunk—"

"Dog!" calls Terence from the doorway.

Arjay looks up and grins at them. "I saw you guys

out there. You should have told me you were coming. I could have got you in free."

Terence shrugs. "Maybe you can score us a refund."

Rat Boy regards Arjay sharply. "Are we boring you, man? We're talking about our future here!"

"We played one set," Arjay reminds him. "Let's not get ahead of ourselves."

To Gecko and Terence, his reluctance is easy to understand. Convicts can't sign recording contracts, and they certainly can't go on tour.

Voodoo tries to smooth things over. "Guitarists. Very high-strung."

The business conversation continues with the original band members, and Arjay goes over to join his roommates.

"You were awesome," Gecko enthuses.

"Thanks. It means a lot that you guys showed up. I really wasn't expecting it. And don't worry about all this manager talk. I won't let it get out of hand."

"We might have another problem," Terence informs him. "You know that chick Casey from group?"

Arjay nods. "I saw her in the audience. I've met her here before. She's into this whole scene."

"Well, now she's your number one fan," Terence continues. "And she's got a mouth on her."

"Gotcha." Arjay looks grim. "She knows we're not supposed to be here, but then again, neither is she. She didn't rat me out last time, but just to be safe, we'd better remind her not to mention anything around Avery."

"*Remind* isn't the word I was thinking of," Terence says darkly.

"What else can we do?" asks Gecko. "We have no control over what she says or doesn't say."

"We can make sure she's so scared of us that she'll be good and careful not to spill the beans about your secret rock star life."

Gecko is wide-eyed. "You mean just threaten her, right? We wouldn't actually do anything."

Terence is growing impatient. "When you threaten, you have to be ready to do something. That's where your whole cred comes from! It's being willing to do something that means you won't have to do it."

"But what if you *do* have to do it?"

"Calm down," Arjay soothes. "We won't see her until next Thursday. Tonight will be ancient history by then."

"In your dreams," Terence sneers. "You're an artist. She wants to frame your used underwear and hang it on her wall."

Sure enough, as they leave Pus Groove via the stage door in the alley, there's Casey, holding up a streetlamp, waiting for them.

She rushes up to Arjay. "Wow! Where do I even start? There's so much I want to ask you!"

Terence steps forward. "Listen, Casey, can I talk to you for a second—"

Arjay puts an iron grip on his shoulder and moves him bodily out of the way.

Terence glares at him. "What are you doing, man? We've got to make sure she understands how it is!"

"I've got it covered," Arjay assures him. He steers Casey away from his roommates and deeper into the alley, where they can have some privacy.

Casey is gushing. "When I saw you here before, I figured it was just a one-time thing! What kind of group home lets you come and go as you please? Join a band? Go to rehearsals and midnight shows?"

In that moment, Arjay realizes that Terence is right. She must be silenced. But he can't see himself following the Florian method. Without even making a conscious decision, he leans forward and presses his lips against hers.

For a second, Casey is shocked. Soon, though, she is kissing him back with real enthusiasm.

From the end of the alley, Terence and Gecko watch in bemused amazement. Terence puts an arm around the smaller boy's shoulders.

"That's another way to plug up a big mouth."

CHAPTER TWENTY-ONE

Gecko is signing the Declaration of Independence. Not as himself—for the purposes of this reenactment, he's William Floyd. He's already been called up as Matthew Thornton. There aren't enough students in fourth-period history to cover all fifty-six signers, so most of them have to double up.

Classmates look over his shoulder as he labors to add eighteenth-century flourishes to the signature, using the unfamiliar fountain pen. Snapple and Chex Mix are being served on the teacher's desk. The girl portraying Ben Franklin is trying to peer through her tiny glasses without going cross-eyed. It isn't exactly a party, but the mood is light, celebratory.

Suddenly, there's dead silence.

Mrs. Garfinkle is in the doorway. Normally, the office summons students by PA or sends a messenger. What's so important that the guidance counselor has to come personally?

Gecko looks up from the Declaration to find all eyes on him. It never takes much for the students of Alma K. Walker to remember who the Social Services kid is.

"Mr. Fosse," beckons the counselor.

He walks down the hall behind her, nervous, but also vaguely miffed at missing the rest of the signing. He's ushered through the outer office into a small conference room. There, seated at the table, is, of all people, Deputy Chief Delancey of the NYPD, munching loudly on a juicy pear.

"Mmm—Gecko. Thanks for coming down. Close the door and have a seat."

Gecko does as he's told, totally at sea. What would the second-in-command of the largest police force in the country want with him?

"How did you find me?" he asks.

The man slurps at his pear. "We know your school, and there's only one Graham who goes by Gecko. Wasn't hard. I'm a cop. That's what we do." He takes another bite and chews noisily. "Funny thing. Roxie thinks you're Gecko Smith. But we know better than that, don't we, Fosse?"

Gecko's insides are ice. He can only nod dumbly. He's spent so much time anticipating the moment when everything falls apart, yet he's never had a sense of what that moment might look like. Is this it—a bald, fruit-slurping cop slapping the cuffs on in a room built for parent-teacher conferences? Are

Healy's three teens headed back to juvie today?

Amazingly, he feels very little pity for himself. He's the one who brought the deputy chief's fateful attention down on them. This is one hundred percent Gecko's fault.

"Fact is, Gecko, I like you. When I saw you looking around that upper-crust aircraft carrier on Sunday, I recognized myself forty years ago—a regular chump getting his first taste of how the other half lives. But Augie Fitzner—*he* doesn't like you. Or maybe he does, but not for his daughter." He pats a file folder on the table in front of him. "And I haven't even told him the good stuff yet—criminal record, halfway house. Quite a rap sheet for a kid your age."

Gecko is completely cowed. He stares at the deputy chief as if he's watching his own executioner sharpening his ax.

"I see you're a man of few words. I like that about you too." He holds out a paper bag. "Pear?"

Gecko shakes his head, silently pleading: *Get on with it—arrest me! Anything's better than being played like a fish on a hook!*

"So," Delancey continues, "be a good Joe and keep away from Roxie, will you?"

Gecko is astonished. *That's* what this is about? Dating a rich guy's daughter? Not the fact that he's one of three juvenile fugitives at large in New York?

"Or I could call this fellow Healy, and you'll be back in Atchison before your next bowel movement, excuse my French. Sure you don't want a pear? They're fresh."

He doesn't know!

The relief that they are not caught floods over Gecko. The big scandal is that August Fitzner's daughter is going out with a halfway-house kid. Nobody looks closely enough to notice that the halfway house itself is kaput, its leader gone, its occupants unsupervised and on the loose.

The relief gives way to a feeling of loss. In the months since Gecko awoke after his accident in the Infiniti, two good things have happened to him—Douglas Healy and Roxanne Fitzner. He's all but destroyed the first. And now he's being forced to give up the second.

He doesn't delude himself. Roxanne may not be his one true love for all time. He's only known her for a few weeks. But his life is not so filled with high points that she doesn't already feature in most of them.

And now that's gone.

"How am I going to tell her?" he manages.

"Smart kid like you, you'll think of something. Just so the father's name never comes up. Or mine. End it nicely, but end it."

He stands and offers his hand, and Gecko shakes it. It's sticky with pear juice.

Gecko isn't sure how long he stays in the conference room after Delancey departs. By the time he gets back to history, the signing is over, and the teacher is unrolling a fresh Declaration of Independence for the next class.

She spies him in the doorway. He must look like the world has just ended. It has.

"Gecko, is everything okay?"

He flees. *Okay?* You have to go back a lot of years before that word is an accurate description of Gecko Fosse. The idea that he actually looked forward to the signing in history fills him with burning shame. How could he be so stupid as to believe that anything *normal* applies to him? Like a dumb class mini-party. Or having a girlfriend.

Briefly, he weighs the idea of dating Roxanne secretly behind her father's back. But the risk—not only for him, but for Arjay and Terence as well. There's too much at stake.

Fifth period is Gecko's lunch. His original plan was to visit the hospital. Now he doesn't want to go. If he doesn't see her, he won't have to break up with her. Then again, not seeing her is the same as being broken up anyway, right?

Since going out with Roxanne, he's been skipping lunch and grabbing snacks between classes—bananas, candy bars, whatever the cafeteria can't screw up. Today, for the first time in weeks, he selects a full lunch. It's his official acknowledgment that the relationship is really over—a paper plate of mac and cheese that looks like grubs smothered in motor oil. Not very appetizing, but still more appealing than the task Deputy Chief Delancey has set for him.

As he scans the big room for a seat, his eyes fall on a curious sight. One minute Diego is carrying his tray to a vacant table. The next he's vanished—now you see him, now you don't. Upon closer inspection, Gecko spots his lab partner on the floor amid the wreckage of his lunch, at the feet of the Goliath who tripped him.

It's been going on all semester, but to Gecko, who has just been pushed around by the second-ranking cop in town, the injustice is suddenly unbearable. Eyes shooting sparks, he storms over, hefts his plate of mac and cheese and pushes it in Goliath's face.

"*Hey!*"

The big kid shakes off the mess, staring in rage and disbelief. By the time Gecko hauls Diego to his feet, a whole pride of Goliaths has materialized behind the original, ready to do battle.

Gecko doesn't care. Ever since fate rescued him from the Atchison laundry room, he's been ahead of the game by one beating, so this will be nothing more than a leveling of his account. No way can these lunkheads dish out anything approaching what the welcoming committee in juvie is capable of.

He stands there, waiting for the punches to start flying, when he notices someone at his side. Terence wears his signature bored expression, but his body language says battle-ready, his posture ramrod straight and defiant.

"Got a problem?" he asks Goliath in a bland tone.

"I got no problem!" is the outraged reply. "Your *dead friend* is the one who's going to have a problem!" He swings at Gecko with a clenched fist, but his posse pulls him back, and the blow whizzes harmlessly in front of its target.

Goliath tears himself free. "What are you doing?"

"Let it go, man," one of the cronies advises.

"Let it go? Did you see what he did?"

Goliath's buddies are reluctant to explain themselves in front of Gecko and Terence, but amid the whispered conversation are words like "juvie," "gangbangers," and "You want to get shot walking home?"

Gecko never could have imagined that the stigma of Social Services and Ms. Vaughn might actually come in handy one day.

Terence plucks a crumpled napkin off the table and offers it to Goliath. "You got noodles in your hair."

Goliath's anger evaporates. He just wants to get out of there. He melts in with his friends, and the group beats a hasty retreat out of the cafeteria.

Diego lets out a tremulous breath. "Thanks."

Gecko can only manage a weak nod, none too steady himself after their near miss. "Terence and me, we're not—you know—we're not what those guys think."

"I know," Diego agrees. "You're a real friend."

"Cut me out of the lovefest," Terence says irritably. "Hey, if I let a bunch of jocks tune up my dog, how's that make me look? Got to protect my cred."

Gecko bites back an annoyed *I'm not your dog*. "Yeah, I wouldn't want to ruin your rep by getting killed," he mumbles. "But thanks anyway."

Besides, the true meaning of this incident has nothing to do with Terence or even Diego. Gecko's lunch—his one excuse for staying away from Yorkville Medical Center—is currently dripping out of a football player's helmet-hair.

Fate is sending him a message: find Roxanne and do what has to be done.

The familiar walk to the hospital seems endless and arduously uphill. Normally, he's so anxious to get there that his feet barely touch the pavement. Today there's little to look forward to.

At the seventh floor he heads straight for room 704, hoping for a long visit. Dr. Radnor is with John Doe, so Gecko hangs back at the door. Doctor and patient are huddled over a laptop computer.

"Get a grip." Gecko feels a light kiss on the back of his neck, and Roxanne is at his side.

"What are they doing?" he asks her.

"Watching old news coverage of 9/11. Dr. Radnor's hoping it'll trigger memories of people in his life at that time."

Karen, a nursing assistant, comes up behind them.

"Roxanne, take Gecko to the laundry and bring back a load of linens. We're running short."

Gecko nearly swallows his lungs. That has always been one of their prime make-out spots. Funny how laundry has become a symbol for the full range of human experience. Misery and dread in Atchison; bliss in the basement of Yorkville Medical Center. And now, amid the roar of industrial-strength washers, with the smell of bleach strong in the air, he has to push away the one person in his life who makes him happy.

Roxanne is setting up a time for them to meet at a movie theater on Saturday, when Gecko suddenly says, "I can't."

"Oh, okay. How about Sunday?"

"No, I mean I can't. Ever."

"What?" She's shocked. "Why not?"

Unable to look her in the eye, he focuses on a spot on the wall over her left shoulder. "Look, Roxanne. I can't do this anymore."

"Go to *movies*?" Then she clues in. "You're *dumping* me?"

He doesn't trust his own voice.

She's upset, but mostly she's just bewildered. "What happened? Is it because of the boat? Because my dad has money?"

Gecko hardens his heart, trying to recapture his old not thinking. It doesn't work. She isn't Reuben, and this is no penny-ante heist. He's hurting her for no reason—at least none that he can give her, which might as well be the same thing.

"Fine." She's speaking to herself as much as Gecko, her agitation spiraling. "This is no big deal! I'm glad it happened!"

"Rox, get a gr—" He stops himself just before it slips out.

"You bastard!" She wheels around and slams a box of powdered detergent into his chest, sending up a cloud of white dust. "Those words *meant* something to me, even if you were just getting your jollies! You can break up with me, but you've forfeited the right to those words from now on!"

She's making no sense, but he nods feebly, because he feels *that* bad. "I really didn't mean it like—"

It's not enough for Roxanne. "Don't talk to me! Don't even look at me! Get out of my hospital!"

And he goes, not even bothering to point out that she doesn't own Yorkville Medical Center. It's entirely possible that Daddy bought it for her.

CHAPTER TWENTY-TWO

Terence slouches against one of the huge concrete supports of the elevated FDR Drive, just in from the East River. His hands are jammed in his pockets against the deepening cold of approaching winter. If Healy was still running things, the group leader would have gotten them winter coats. But there's no point in woulda, shoulda, coulda. Anyway, if tonight goes well, it won't be long before Terence can afford the warmest coat in New York. Mink, even.

He betrays no discomfort, though, or even the excitement that everything he's worked for is about to come through. It's all about attitude when dealing with a guy like DeAndre. Show any weakness and you're doomed.

DeAndre ambles onto the scene, fashionably late by half an hour. He's accompanied by four of his crew. Terence recognizes a couple of faces from school. Nobody's smiling, but that's part of the game. Terence isn't either.

"So what's the story?" Terence opens. "Are we doing business, or what?"

The razor-cut dollar sign stands out in stark contrast in the harsh glare of the streetlight.

"Don't know what you're talking about, yo," DeAndre drawls. "I don't do business with anybody but my crew."

"Yeah, right," Terence says sarcastically. "I saw that when you jacked *my* iPods! Or maybe that doesn't count because I got stiffed on my own plan!"

DeAndre scowls. "You got a point, make it."

"I put money in your pocket. I could put a lot more. I've earned a place with your crew."

There's some discontented mumbling from the group, which DeAndre quells with a single look. To Terence he says, "You think this is some rich-boy fraternity where you learn the secret handshake and you're in?"

Terence permits himself a ghost of a smile. If DeAndre has allowed the conversation to get to this stage, he's already decided to let Terence in. The only question is what he wants in return.

"All right, no handshake. What's the cover charge?"

DeAndre nods approvingly. "Didn't I tell you he was sharp?"

The five lead Terence a few blocks north to where

a group of homeless people huddle around a trash-can fire. On the river side of the roadway is a tiny park, barely a city block, with a children's playground and a fountain.

At first glance, the place is deserted. But on closer examination, Terence can see a lone bag lady snoozing on a bench. Her grocery cart stands guard beside her, filled with soda cans and other random junk.

"Meet Pauline," DeAndre announces. "She's bugging so bad, even the homeless keep their distance."

"Yeah, yeah," Terence interrupts impatiently. "Life's cruel. So what?"

"So that's your initiation. Take the old girl, tune her up a little, load her in the cart, and dump her in the fountain."

Terence grins appreciatively. "No problem. You want me to take her to City Hall and marry her before I put her in the drink?"

"Pay attention, yo," DeAndre reproves. "She wears a ring on her left hand—says it's her high school ring from back in the day. Bring it to me after—proof the job is done."

Terence's smirk disappears abruptly as he realizes DeAndre is serious. "What are you talking about, man? She's just a crazy old bag. Why would you want anybody to mess with her?"

The razor-cut boy's expression hardens. "Not so gangster now, huh? Think you've got a place in this crew if you're afraid to get your hands dirty?"

"I do what needs to be done," Terence insists angrily. "Get me on a score, and you've never seen anybody hold his end up better. But this is for nothing! There's no green in it. Risk without reward, man—that's not business."

"My business is to look out for my crew," DeAndre snarls. "Can we trust you? Maybe, maybe not. But we trust you better if we've got something on you. And we'll know you're no cop."

"You've already got something on me," Terence reasons. "I took that iPod from you—receiving stolen goods, B felony. You don't need this."

DeAndre is adamant. "I didn't come looking for you. You came looking for me."

A sick feeling comes over Terence, and he struggles to maintain his bravado. From the moment he was old enough to realize that his father was a jerk with a mean streak, he's understood that the solution is to get with a solid crew. When you're down with the right people, you've got it all—respect, protection, money. Nobody messes with you, and when you want something, you call on your dogs to make it happen.

His mind revisits his very first day at Alma K. Walker—DeAndre, fencing cell phones in the can.

I thought DeAndre was that guy for me in New York.

Watching Pauline snooze beside her grocery cart in that parkette, he knows he was very wrong.

He turns to the razor-cut boy. "Forget it, man. I

thought you were interested in scoring some green."

DeAndre's perma-frown turns ugly. "Maybe where you come from there's do-overs, but this isn't something you take back. Either she's going in the fountain or you are."

Involuntarily, Terence retreats a step.

DeAndre is triumphant. "You're *nothing*! You're all about picking locks and snatch and grab. But you can't handle the heat that comes with it. It's a package deal, yo. That's something you're going to learn tonight." He nods at his henchmen, and they advance menacingly.

The *blurp* of a police siren shatters the quiet. A single squad car crawls along the lower roadway and pulls up to the homeless people and their fire.

DeAndre and his crew melt away, but not before the razor-cut boy issues a final warning: "You've got the weekend. Bring me the ring on Monday to prove it's done." The snake eyes narrow to slits. "The fountain closes for winter; the river's open all year."

They scatter.

CHAPTER TWENTY-THREE

The cake reads GOOD LUCK, VICTORIA, and Dr. Avery is struggling to cut it with a plastic knife. Metal cutlery is banned for any mental health provider that receives state funding. There's none in apartment 4B either.

It's a party for Victoria Ko, who is officially graduating from the group that day.

"I'm very proud of what you've accomplished," Dr. Avery tells her. "But I have to admit, I'll miss you."

"I'll miss you guys too," Victoria says emotionally. "Especially you, Dr. Avery. You've helped me so much. I brought you a little thank-you present."

The psychotherapist looks stricken. "Oh, thanks. Uh—you shouldn't have." She removes the wrapping paper like a sapper approaching unexploded ordnance. The gift is a Gucci scarf of fine silk that would have set a purchaser back several hundred dollars.

"Nice," grumbles Drew Roddenbury. "The record companies are going to have me here till I'm seventy, and *she's* cured? Give me a break."

"Drew," the doctor scolds gently. "You know the first rule of group. Nobody is judged here, and we're *never* hurtful to one another."

"Oh yeah, right," Casey mutters sarcastically.

Dr. Avery turns to her. "Has someone in this group been unkind to you?"

"*Hello!* He didn't even call!" The punk rock girl makes a face at Arjay.

Arjay looks stunned. "I don't have your number."

"Ever heard of four-one-one?" she shoots back.

The doctor steps in. "Now, I understand that at your age, people are going to develop feelings for each other. But we must never act on them."

"Yeah, well, you should have told that to Don Juan on steroids."

Dr. Avery's eyes shoot sparks. "Do you mean to tell me that you two have been involved romantically while coming to group?"

The "No!" from Arjay is so plaintive and high-pitched that it seems like the cry of a small child.

"You can say that again!" Casey snorts. "No room for that in his retarded preadolescent rock star fantasy."

Gecko's coughing fit draws everyone's attention, as it was meant to do.

But the therapist has already picked up on the two fateful words. "Rock star?"

"Joey Ramone visits the Big and Tall shop is more like it!"

Dr. Avery's eyebrows disappear into her perfect hairline. "You—you're in a band?" she asks Arjay. "And Mr. Healy doesn't object?"

"He hasn't said a word against it," Arjay replies carefully.

Her finely drawn features contract into an expression of perplexity. At last she says, "Please ask Mr. Healy to give me a call at his earliest convenience. I'm not sure I've got a handle on what your schedule is like."

The walk home is very tense after group therapy ends at six o'clock.

"Schedule," Gecko repeats nervously. "I think that means how does a halfway-house kid with school, community service, and group manage to find time to be in a band."

"You should have let me handle Casey," growls Terence in disgust.

"What were you going to do—shoot her?" Arjay challenges.

"I wouldn't have kissed her, that's for sure! One round of tonsil hockey, and she's psycho 'cause you dissed her. Was it worth it, Casanova? This girlfriend thing is the third rail! I told Romeo the same when he started dating the First National Bank of Whatsername."

Gecko looks grim. "Well, you don't have to worry

about that anymore. It's history. Daddy doesn't approve of me."

Arjay glares at Terence. "I had to kiss her. I couldn't leave her in the hands of a goon like you."

Terence grabs the bigger boy and wheels him around. "You know nothing about me, man! You killed somebody, and *I'm* a goon? I'm in a lot of trouble, and you know why? Because I'm *not* a goon!"

Arjay is instantly alert. "What trouble?"

Terence clams up. "Don't worry about it. My problem."

"Your problem *is* our problem," puts in Gecko. "What happens to one of us happens to everybody."

"I'm supposed to tune up this old bag lady and toss her in a fountain, where she'll probably drown or die of hypothermia," Terence confesses.

Gecko is horrified. "Why?"

"It's DeAndre, man. I've been trying to get with his crew. Don't look at me like that! I'm not doing it! And if I say no, I'm the next victim."

Arjay's face flames red. "And I'm stupid because I kissed a girl? God, Terence, what's so important about finding some criminals to hang out with? You've been obsessed with that dirtbag since the first day of school!"

Terence tries to explain. "Don't you get it? I'm not like you guys! Yeah, you're convicts too. But mostly by accident—bad luck. When all this is over, you're going to be model citizens. For a guy like me, getting with a good crew is the only place to be! It's like an insurance policy that nothing bad's going to happen."

"That's bull, and you know it!" Arjay exclaims. "You had your own crew in Chicago, and look what it did for you. You got yourself locked up, same as us."

Terence looks away. For a moment he studies the facade of the brownstone they're passing. Finally, he mumbles, "Maybe it wasn't exactly like what I said."

"Oh, right," Gecko sneers. "Healy pulled you out of Mensa, not juvie."

"That's not what I mean."

Arjay is clueing in. "There was no crew, was there?"

"There was a crew. Evergreen Southside. My old man is a mean streak hooked up to a fifty-kilowatt speaker. You hear his big mouth a block and a half away: 'You're a loser!' 'He's a moron!' 'She's a cow!' Except when those Southsiders are around. Then it's like he's at church. Not a peep. God, I wanted to be one of those guys!" He lapses into a melancholy silence.

"What happened?" Gecko prompts.

Terence's voice is barely audible. "They wouldn't let me in. I got good at everything they were good at—better than them. I was a one-man crime wave. Chicago PD doubled foot patrols in the neighborhood, but I was in the zone. I could break into maximum-security lockup and jack the warden's false teeth. Not good enough for the Southsiders. 'Take a hike, kid.'"

"A gangster without a gang," Arjay muses.

"Don't rub it in, man."

"So what happened?" Gecko probes.

"I had to show them what I had to offer. I put together a score they couldn't resist—planned the whole job for them."

"And you got caught," Gecko concludes.

"Worse. They pulled it themselves—cut me out, then turned me in to the cops. That was my ticket to juvie."

"And you did the same thing with DeAndre," Arjay says wearily. "Man, don't you learn from experience?"

"I guess not," Terence mutters. "I guess it's too much to ask for to get down with some dogs like everybody else."

"Will you speak English for once?" Arjay explodes. "What about Gecko and me? *We're* your dogs! You talk about a crew—we're the tightest crew that ever existed! We're together because we're all screwed! We couldn't let DeAndre mess with you even if we wanted to. If the cops pick you up with a fractured skull, they'll figure out who you are, and we *all* go down. We've got your back because we have no choice!"

They're standing in front of their building now. Arjay lets them in the front door and then rushes to help Mrs. Liebowitz, who is sweeping the stairs.

She awards them a semi-smile and looks pointedly behind them at the empty space where Douglas Healy should be.

"He's in meetings all day," Arjay supplies quickly.

"He certainly trusts you," she comments.

"That's because we're trustworthy, Mrs. L."

She nods. "You're a good boy, Arjay. And those two are probably also okay—except maybe him." She indicates Terence.

"He's a good boy too," Arjay assures her.

"I was very hard on you three when you first moved in, and I'm sorry." She peers intently at them. "Am I wrong to be sorry?"

"No, ma'am. You're not wrong."

Once inside Apartment 4B, they begin to breathe again.

"She's not going to hold off forever," Gecko comments. "She wants to know where Healy is."

"We just have to keep our heads," Arjay insists. "There's nothing we can't handle if we stick together and don't do anything stupid." He hits the button on the telephone answering machine.

"Mr. Healy, it's Debra Vaughn from Social Services. I'm sorry I haven't been able to get around to you sooner, but my caseload hasn't allowed it. I will be there on Wednesday at nine a.m. for my evaluation. I've let the school know that the boys will be missing their morning classes. Your reports have been exemplary. Let's hope they represent the true state of affairs."

When the beep sounds to end the recording, all three of them jump.

Wednesday. Six days.

CHAPTER TWENTY-FOUR

Gecko has been to the hospital many times, but this is a first for Arjay and Terence, who never made it past the emergency room door on the night of Healy's accident.

As they ride up in the elevator, Terence is relentless about the surname on Gecko's volunteer badge. "Smith—real creative. How long did that brainstorm take you?"

"Like you could do better," snaps Gecko.

"I know hamsters who could do better."

"Knock it off," orders Arjay.

It sounds like light banter, but there's nothing light about the mission that has brought them here. Ms. Vaughn's message has placed a time bomb inside a structure that has already begun to collapse.

Mrs. Liebowitz likes them now, but her suspicions over Healy's absence are growing stronger. Dr. Avery is expecting a call from the group leader that she's obviously not going to get. This Page Cannot Be Displayed is anxious to sign with their new manager, and the members are demanding a social security number that Arjay refuses to provide. The Deputy Chief of Police of the City of New York has Gecko's file on his desk—all the information he needs to sink them if he bothers to check a few facts. Add to that DeAndre, who will be coming after Terence sooner or later, with who knows what results.

Their Wednesday date with Ms. Vaughn may be the worst of their problems, but it's only hastening the inevitable.

With total disaster less than a week away, they have no choice but to try for a miracle. That's what they're doing in the hospital today.

The plan is to walk in on John Doe and come completely clean about who they are and who he is. Maybe the combination of the trio together, plus the truth, will trigger the return of the group leader's memory. And then maybe—an even bigger maybe—he'll forgive them and cover for them.

"And if he doesn't," Terence concludes, "I hope you've been practicing yoga, because it's time to bend over and kiss our butts good-bye."

"What's the worst that can happen?" Arjay challenges. "He calls the cops and we get arrested. That's in the mail for Wednesday anyway."

They step out onto the seventh floor and Gecko waves his tag in front of the security door. Down the hall they march, single file, Gecko in the lead. After spending every spare moment in this place, he hasn't been here since his breakup with Roxanne four days ago. Every lunch tray, every IV pole, every molecule of antiseptic-smelling air reminds him of that last ugly fight. And it hurts.

The procession comes to a halt in front of room 704. With a collective intake of breath, the trio walks inside. They stare. They goggle. They are strangled and silent.

The man in the bed, fast asleep, is an elderly Asian.

Only Terence can access his speech center. "Unless he's changed a lot . . ." His voice trails off.

"Did he *die*?" Arjay manages.

"He was totally fine except for his memory!" Gecko insists, his voice rising with panic.

"Oh, hi, Gecko." Karen, the nursing assistant, comes in with some fresh towels. "I suppose you're looking for your John Doe. He transferred out yesterday."

"He's cured?" Gecko whispers.

She shakes her head sadly. "Physically, he's healthy, so we can't keep him in an acute care facility. It's too bad, really. He has no money or insurance, so in the city system, he goes somewhere they have mental health experts."

"Where's that?" Gecko asks in alarm.

She hesitates. "The only bed they had open was in the Bronx County Psychiatric Hospital."

Terence is horrified. "He's in the *nuthouse*?"

She looks guilt-ridden. "Well, there was nowhere else . . . he'll be receiving the best . . . yes," she admits finally.

"*How could you let that happen?*" Gecko howls.

Arjay steps in front of him. "Calm down. It isn't her fault."

True. You can't blame a nursing assistant for a patient transfer. Even the doctors and hospital administrators wouldn't have the power to overrule the city system. No, responsibility for this lies squarely with the teenagers who could have identified Healy but didn't, because they were more worried about their own problems.

Karen hangs her head. "Sorry, Gecko. Everybody knew you'd be upset, but we had no way to get in touch with you. He asked about you a bunch of times. Roxanne told us you dropped out of the volunteers. Is that true?"

Gecko studies his sneakers. "Sort of. I guess so."

"Well, he's totally okay. He just has to stay there until his memory comes back." She touches his arm. "I hope that's really soon. They say it's not the nicest place."

Gecko can barely put one foot in front of the other as they slink to the stairwell for an emergency powwow. A force is pressing down on him, but he can't tell where gravity ends and despair begins. So much has happened, yet this latest twist is surely the cruelest.

Arjay takes a deep breath. "Okay, let's think this through."

"Think it through?" Gecko explodes. "The only person who ever cared about us is in a mental hospital, and it's *all our fault*!"

"Hey," Terence says sharply. "We don't have the juice to commit anybody to anything. This just happened. Lousy luck, man, that's it."

"What are you, on drugs?" Gecko demands in a fury. "We could have given ourselves up the night of his accident. We didn't. We could have identified him the minute he was diagnosed with amnesia. We didn't. We could have come forward the whole time he was in this hospital. We didn't."

"We *couldn't*," Terence amends. "Not without scoring ourselves a one-way ticket to lockup."

"Yeah, well, maybe we should be thinking beyond what's best for us, you self-centered bloodsucker!"

"We can still come forward," Arjay points out. "They think Healy has no money or insurance, but he probably does somewhere. They can't hold him if he's got a life to return to—even if he can't remember that life."

"And we go back inside," Terence adds, "with time tacked on for fun and games in NYC. Assault, fleeing custody, falsifying reports—who knows what the cops'll come up with? Attempted murder, maybe."

"You think I'm thrilled about it?" Arjay demands. "At least you guys go to juvie. For me it's real jail!"

Gecko nods. "So that's it, then. We sacrifice

ourselves to save Healy. It's no more than he did for us. Fair trade."

"Fair trade, bite me," Terence snaps. "Not until we've tried everything else."

"There's nothing else to try," Arjay reasons wearily. "We always knew this couldn't last forever. We go back into the system on Wednesday anyway. We're just pushing it up a few days."

"You're ignoring the most obvious thing," Terence insists. "Let's find this rat hole where they put Healy and bust him out."

Gecko stares at him. "It's a hospital for crazy people! You think you can come and go as you please?"

"I may not be the bomb at school, or following rules, or being a good citizen, but there's stuff I know how to do. Like breaking and entering."

"That's not the same as busting out," Arjay reminds him.

Terence shrugs. "So I'll do it backward. Seriously, what's the worst that can happen? We get caught, and confess *then*. But if we spring him, we've got a shot at convincing him to cover for us."

"You're dreaming," Gecko accuses. "It'll never happen in a million years."

"Maybe you're right," Terence agrees. "But there's a *chance*. Some chance against no chance—who wouldn't take those odds?"

They turn to Arjay to cast the deciding vote. The big boy throws up his arms. "Where's the Bronx?"

CHAPTER TWENTY-FIVE

The Bronx, it turns out, is at the other end of a thirty-minute ride on the Number 4 train. The trio emerges from the subway entrance into the shadow of a hulking gray monstrosity that might be the ugliest building in the city. The Bronx County Psychiatric Hospital is a fourteen-story gray stone cube. The only decorative features are the iron bars on the windows—no designs, no columns, no ornamentation, and not a speck of color anywhere. It looks like exactly what it is—a very large trash receptacle for those New Yorkers considered too crazy to be let loose among the population.

And Douglas Healy.

Arjay emits a low whistle. "You know when they say, 'find a happy place'? Well, this isn't it."

Terence shrugs. "I've seen worse."

Getting inside the building is no problem, but once there, security is tight. An armed guard watches over the reception desk. Visitors wait in line to pass through an airport-style metal detector. The patient wards are sequestered behind the same kind of armored door they have at Atchison. A sick feeling of déjà vu takes hold in Gecko's gut. To be admitted, you have to be buzzed in by a white-coated attendant.

Getting Healy out of here is not going to be easy.

"Yes?"

They jump. The woman at reception is looking them over through the bulletproof glass, her expression steely.

"What's up?" Terence greets her conversationally. "A friend of ours just got transferred here. Figured we'd look in on him, make sure he's doing okay."

"His name?" she barks.

"John Doe," Gecko supplies quickly. The New York City health system has never heard of Douglas Healy.

She regards them suspiciously. "Your friend is a John Doe?"

Sweat beads on Gecko's brow. "I'm a volunteer at Yorkville Medical. I got to know him in the head trauma unit down there." He shows her his Gecko Smith ID badge.

From a drawer she produces a sheaf of printed forms and slides them through an opening in the glass divider. "Fill these out."

Gecko accepts the stack, frowning at its thickness. "And then we go in?"

Wordlessly, she points to a sign: ALL VISITS MUST BE APPROVED IN ADVANCE.

Arjay speaks up. "Uh—how far in advance?"

"The applications go up to Albany at the end of the day. Then, if you pass the background check—figure about a week."

The mood out on the sidewalk is panic to the third power.

"We don't have a week!" Gecko babbles. "The dragon lady is coming in four days!"

Arjay is also shaken. "We'd never pass the background check anyway. There's no way we're going to get in there. It's just not possible."

The words have barely passed his lips when the automatic doors slide open and a petite blonde steps out.

Gecko's eyes bulge. "*Rox?*"

He can almost feel the cold blast as her recognition turns to icy anger, her open, friendly features freezing into a countenance of disdain. "You," she barely whispers.

Gecko doesn't defend himself. He doesn't deserve defending. Besides, he's missed her these past few days. Roxanne's rage is still better than no Roxanne at all.

"You never even gave me your phone number," she mutters resentfully. "How stupid am I?"

He reaches for her. "You're not stupid—"

She pushes him away. "Oh, I'm a genius. Straight A's in a top school, and I'm still dumb enough to think you like me when you don't even want me to call. What, you're afraid your *real* girlfriend might pick up the phone?"

"It wasn't like that—"

Her voice rises in tone and volume. "Selfish jerk, I had no way to tell you about John Doe!"

"It's okay—"

"It's *not* okay!" she storms. "Look what they've done to him! It's so—so *sad* to see him in there!"

"Hold on." Terence puts two and two together. "*She's* your girlfriend? Dog, I'm impressed! I always figured a little dweeb like you, no offense—"

"Roxanne, meet Terence and Arjay," Gecko introduces them.

"Wait a minute!" Arjay cuts to the chase. "You *saw* John Doe? How did you get in? They told us it takes a week to get approved."

"My dad has contacts in the police department. He might be able to get you guys in too. I'll call him." She takes out her cell phone.

"It's not a good idea," Gecko says quickly.

"You're John's closest friend. He *needs* to see you."

"No!" he exclaims more forcefully than he intended.

"Why not?"

"Because your dad can't know you're talking to me! Listen—Delancey came to my school. He said he'd make big trouble for me if I didn't break up with you."

She's mystified. "Why would he do that?"

"Don't you get it? Your dad sent him. He doesn't think I'm good enough for you! And he's right!"

Her face flushes red, and she dials the cell phone, punching angrily at the keypad.

Gecko snatches it away from her. "He can't find out I told you! That was another part of the deal. You're not supposed to know he's behind it!"

She glares at him. "Thanks for standing up for me. I'm glad I mean so much to you."

"Come on—a millionaire and a police chief?" Gecko defends himself. "What was I supposed to do?"

"It's a free country," she says resentfully. "What did they offer you? Money? How's the pay for dumping someone who really, *really* likes you? How much am I worth?"

Gecko turns to Arjay and Terence, who nod. The secrecy has gone on for so long that it feels like part of the fabric of reality. But it's time for the truth.

He regards her intently. "Promise you'll listen to the whole story before calling the cops."

She's genuinely alarmed now. "You're scaring me, Gecko. What's going on?"

He takes a deep breath. "John Doe isn't really a John Doe. His name is Douglas Healy, and he's the only thing standing between the three of us and jail."

Her eyes widen in amazement as Gecko recounts the story: three young inmates; a second chance, thanks to Healy; then a terrible accident on the fire escape.

She's horrified. "And you kept your mouth shut while he got sent *here*?"

"It wasn't supposed to go this far!" Gecko pleads. "Radnor kept saying his memory would come back!"

"And it might have—if you just told the guy who he is! Instead you let him go on thinking—God, who knows what he could be thinking?"

"We had no choice," Arjay puts in gently. "What if we exposed ourselves and he still didn't remember?"

"Then you'd have the satisfaction of doing the right thing for the man who helped you," she says sharply.

"But would it have been the right thing?" Arjay argues. "Healy wanted us out of jail. He basically devoted his whole life to setting up the halfway house. If we get arrested, we'll be undoing everything he worked for."

"Oh, that's rich!" She turns to Gecko. "Where'd you find this guy? He'll make a great lawyer someday."

"Step off," Terence says protectively. "We're trying to do the stand-up thing here."

Roxanne is suspicious. "What stand-up thing?"

"We're not here to visit," Gecko tells her. "We're looking for a way to bust Healy out." He explains about the Wednesday meeting with Ms. Vaughn that has set them on a collision course with disaster. "Our only hope is to get him home and try to jump-start his memory ourselves."

"And if you're caught?" she demands.

"We confess everything," Arjay promises. "Either way, Healy ends up okay."

"For him, it's only a few extra days," Gecko adds. "For us, it could be all the difference in the world. A chance to stay out of jail. A life versus no life."

"I'll help," she says suddenly.

"Rox—no!" Gecko exclaims. "We can't ask that! We're already in trouble—you're squeaky clean!"

"That's why you need me," she argues. "I can get inside! I'll ask my dad to get my volunteer work switched *here*. I can be your eyes—I'll give you the layout, so you can find a way in."

Gecko is blown away. "You'd do that for us?"

"I'd do it for *you*. I can't believe what my father put you through. And we both owe it to your friend Mr. Healy."

Terence shoots Gecko an approving nod. "She's got it going on, dog. Maybe I should give this girlfriend gig a second look."

CHAPTER TWENTY-SIX

As an amnesia patient at Yorkville Medical Center, John Doe was convinced that things could not possibly be worse.

He was wrong.

Purgatory. There's no nicer word to describe Bronx County Psychiatric Hospital. For any sane person to be committed to an asylum is the ultimate form of torture.

"You haven't been committed," Dr. Peterson explains patiently. "This is just where the system, in its infinite wisdom, has put you until your memory comes back."

Until your memory comes back. He's heard those words before. There's only one problem. It isn't happening.

"So I'm free to walk out of here any time I please?"

The doctor favors him with a sympathetic smile. "It's a little more complicated than that, I'm afraid. You haven't been committed here by the state, but this *is* a secure facility. And that security doesn't distinguish between you and anybody else."

"*My tickets!*" comes a bellow behind them.

An obese man with shoulder-length gray hair is shaking a younger patient by the shoulders. Instantly, two white-coated attendants grab the attacker and pull him away.

"But he's got my tickets!"

"Time for your meds, Hugo," grunts one of the attendants, restraining the much bigger man.

"Sorry you had to see that," Peterson apologizes, as the white coats drag Hugo off to the nurses' station.

"See it?" Healy says bitterly. "You can set your watch by it. He's fine till the Zoloft wears off. Sometime around *Judge Judy* he starts freaking out because he can't find his floor seats for the Black Sabbath show they have *every night*!"

"Perhaps he's gained weight," the doctor muses, "so his regular dose is no longer sufficient—"

"The point is, I don't belong here," Healy interrupts impatiently. "This place is for real mental illness. I'm just a guy who got hit on the head. I don't even have a concussion anymore."

"It's only temporary," Peterson says gently. "As soon as your memory returns—"

"What if it *never* returns?"

"There's no reason to believe that will be the case," the doctor soothes. "It's extremely rare."

"But not impossible," Healy argues. "What then?"

Dr. Peterson has no answer, just like Dr. Radnor

before him. At a certain point there's nothing left to say. Bronx Psych may be awful, but if these people discharge Healy tomorrow, where could he go? A homeless shelter? Doesn't he have a better chance of building some sort of life for himself if he stays put and waits it out?

So he's stuck here. But for how long? The total absence of any answer looms like an endless black void. Hugo and his concert tickets are the least of it. Some of these people are seriously nuts—like Stefan, whose facial tick is so severe that he's a human bobble-head, nodding and shaking until he finally makes himself seasick and throws up.

My God, I feel for him—it's not his fault, but where do I fit in with a guy like that?

Or Con Ed, who refuses to go to bed because he's convinced that, at midnight, the power company drains all the energy from his body. Besides Healy, the sanest person in the building is the mob guy who was found not guilty by reason of insanity. Even in his case, it's impossible to tell if he's a gangster pretending to be a mental patient, or a mental patient who's delusional about being a gangster. All Healy has to go on are his stories of contract hits and truck hijackings and his colorful threats of what he'll do to anybody who squeals on him.

The staff is nice enough, but they're harassed and busy. No one has the inclination for a normal conversation. At any moment an attendant might have to run off and prevent someone from painting the walls with tomato juice or attacking Wolf Blitzer on a TV screen.

Besides, they're *strangers*. What a stupid thing to say. In his condition, who isn't a stranger? Yet that might be the hardest part of this. Thanks to his amnesia, the people at Yorkville make up everybody he knows in the world. The only person he recognizes here is Roxanne. When he first saw her in the common room, he actually ran over and hugged her—that's how much emotion is generated by a familiar face.

"What are you doing here?"

"My volunteer assignment got changed," she explains. "Small world, huh?"

"Yeah, but a nice kid like you in a place like this?"

She smiles. "This is where I'm needed. You see a bad place; I see somewhere I can do the most good."

What a sweetheart. The fact that she's going to be around makes the future a tiny bit less bleak. But even she has little time for him now. She's busy with orientation, learning about the facility, and her new responsibilities.

He doesn't ask her about Gecko, because he knows the two are on the outs. Too bad. That's another quality teenager. A little odd, to be sure, with his quiet intensity. But a great kid, nonetheless.

It doesn't matter. Chances are, he's never going to lay eyes on the boy again.

He sighs glumly. *How many people have I let go of already—without even knowing it?*

CHAPTER TWENTY-SEVEN

The meeting is set for Sal's Famous—Healy's favorite pizza place. Even in his absence, the group leader's influence hangs over them.

"Hope your girl likes pepperoni," Terence mumbles, tying into his second slice.

"I have no idea what food she likes or doesn't like," Gecko says honestly. "I never took her out to eat. How could I? We had next to no cash and no idea how long we had to make it last."

Arjay wraps his mouth around a king-size bite. "Well, we don't have to worry about that anymore. One way or another, we know exactly how long our money has to last. Till Wednesday. After that, we'll either have Healy paying our bills again, or we'll be accepting the hospitality of the Department of Corrections."

Terence glances nervously at the clock on the wall. "Where's your chick, Gecko? Think she might stiff us?"

"She has to make sure she's not followed," Gecko

explains. "If her old man's crazy enough to send the deputy chief of police to scare me away, who's to say he wouldn't keep an eye on her too?"

As he speaks, Roxanne appears in the fly-specked glass of the front door and enters the pizzeria. He can actually feel himself flush. He's embarrassed by how happy he is to see her. The rush even wipes out for a moment the all-pervading dread of what they have to do, and the fate that awaits them if they can't make it work.

"Man, she looks *good*," comments Terence in a low voice. "Still can't figure out what she's doing with you."

Arjay is sober. "Let's just concentrate on what she has to say."

Roxanne slides into the booth beside Gecko. "Sorry I'm late, you guys. The whole hospital was in lockdown because they couldn't find one of the patients on the eighth floor."

Gecko is instantly alert. "He escaped?"

"No, he tried to put all his clothes on at the same time and wedged himself in the closet. But they weren't letting anybody in or out until they found him." Her face darkens. "They're very serious about security up there. It would have been a lot easier to get your friend Healy out of Yorkville."

"No point in moaning about that now," Arjay puts in. "How much of the hospital have you had the chance to see?"

"Most of it, I think—wow, pepperoni! My favorite." She picks up a slice. "The orientation is a huge deal. They run the hospital like a jail, and keeping the patients inside is Job One. That's the first thing the head nurse told me."

Terence is not a believer. "These places—they talk big security, but it's hot air. You can get into anywhere. Something—a skylight, a window—"

She shakes her head. "The windows are barred, and there are no skylights. I thought about the roof, but the access is locked and chained. Besides, you'd have to be Spider-Man to get in that way. We're the tallest building for three blocks."

"What about fire exits?" Arjay suggests.

"They're all outside main security," she tells him. "And there's no way to pull the fire alarm and disappear in the confusion. Each patient is assigned to a fire marshal, and there's a disaster plan they practice every month. Not to mention the police station around the corner. During lockdown today, the cops were there in, like, thirty seconds. It's a lost cause, guys. Maybe you should just confess."

Terence is scornful. "Confess, nothing! A building like that doesn't run by itself. They need deliveries—food, toilet paper, those gowns that don't cover your butt, whatever! Where do they take out the garbage? Not through the metal detector at the front door, that's for sure!"

She looks thoughtful. "There's a lane in the back of the building, leading up to the loading docks. All deliveries come in there, and that's where they put out the garbage. But there's a guard post blocking the alley. Everybody going in or out has to be authorized by the desk."

Terence is concentrating hard. "Twenty-four hours a day?"

"I don't think so," she replies. "Last night when I left, the guard hut was empty. But the gate was padlocked shut."

A big grin splits Terence's face. "The lock doesn't exist that can keep me out."

Arjay speaks up. "Maybe Rox could go to the loading dock and let us inside."

She shakes her head. "That's all closed up at night. Terence can pick a lock, but I can't."

Their faces fall. Just when it seems like they've found a way in, there's another dead end.

Then Roxanne says, "Unless . . ." Their eyes are on her again, wide and pleading. ". . . there's a small door off the kitchen, leading to the Dumpsters. It's locked to the outside. But someone on the inside could open it for you."

Never before have Gecko and Arjay seen Terence so businesslike. For the next twenty minutes he questions Roxanne on the minutest details of the alley, the kitchen, the layout of that part of the hospital, and the people who work there. If the kid would devote this kind of energy and drive to schoolwork, he'd be a presidential scholar.

As the plan crystallizes, Gecko's heart begins to

pound. Calm down, he cautions himself. The odds against us are a million to one.

Pull the breakout, bring back Healy's memory, convince him to cover for them with Ms. Vaughn. A long shot? Try no shot! And yet when the whole scheme is broken down into single steps, not one of them is impossible.

Gecko asks the practical question. "When?"

"Tomorrow," Terence replies matter-of-factly. "How many days do you think we've got?"

"That's perfect," Roxanne puts in. "I work till eight, and I can tell my parents I'm sleeping at a friend's house. Then, when I do get home, I'll just say there was a change of plan."

Gecko feels a pang of remorse. "No wonder your dad doesn't want you to have anything to do with me. Look at what I've got you mixed up in."

She slips her hand into his and shrugs, smiling. "Get a grip."

How he's missed those three words.

Terence puts his two cents in. "You want Arjay and me to scram so you guys can make all these people lose their appetites?"

Gecko and Roxanne move apart self-consciously.

"Anyway," Arjay concludes, "tonight's not the time for celebrating. Tomorrow night."

Maybe.

Nobody speaks it, but the word hangs there as clearly as if it's been broadcast in the pizzeria.

They say good-bye to Roxanne and trudge back down Third Avenue toward Ninety-seventh Street. They make a very quiet procession, each one anticipating a sleepless night and a tortured day. Gecko suffers doubly, knowing that he has just passed up what might well be his last chance to kiss Roxanne. Tomorrow night, in the heat of the breakout, there will be no time for that. And afterward, it's more than likely he'll never see her again.

"What's up, yo?"

Arjay already has his key in the lock when the shadowy figures appear behind them. Four hang back. When the fifth steps forward, the razor-cut dollar sign gleams in the lamplight.

Arjay moves away from the door and regards DeAndre. "Something I can do for you, pal?"

DeAndre looks the massive Arjay up and down. "This is between me and the yo, here."

"I'm not doing it," Terence says firmly. "It doesn't make me feel like a gangster to dump an old lady into a frozen puddle. Guess I haven't got what it takes to be with your crew."

DeAndre shakes his head. "That's not how it works. You're on the hook for this. No backing out."

Terence sighs. "No disrespect—I don't have time for this, man."

The snake eyes narrow. "I didn't ask for it. You did."

Terence tries to be reasonable. "Things change, DeAndre."

"Not *this* thing! I'm not your hobby. What you start with me, you finish. Or there's payback." His four crew members step into the light.

Arjay and Gecko move forward to flank Terence. With all that they have on their plate, a brawl is the last thing they need. But they can't leave Terence to face them alone.

Out of the darkness above, a cascade of water splatters on the sidewalk, drenching DeAndre and his crew. Shocked, the razor-cut teen stares at Terence, searching for the weapon his adversary used to call down a deluge from the heavens. When he finally looks up, he spies Mrs. Liebowitz leaning out her window, an empty saucepan in one hand, her cell phone in the other.

"I've dialed nine-one-one and I'm about to push the send button! You get out of here and leave my boys alone!"

DeAndre glares at Terence. "Twenty-four hours, yo. Get it done or *you* get done!" He and his crew storm off down the street, shoes squishing on the pavement.

Arjay looks up to thank Mrs. Liebowitz, but the window is already shut.

"They'll be back," Terence predicts bleakly. "Count on it."

Arjay takes a deep breath. "We've got bigger problems than those guys."

"Maybe so," says Gecko with a shiver. "But now they know where we live."

CHAPTER TWENTY-EIGHT

Roxanne Fitzner signs her duty chart, shrugs out of her hospital lab coat, and tosses it into the laundry bin in the staff lounge.

She draws an anxious breath. Her shift is over, but her night is just beginning. Brushing aside the fear that she might be too scared to do what she has to do, she steps out into the corridor.

"Hi, Roxanne. How are you fitting in?"

One of the orderlies, Gerard Somebody.

"Loving it," she replies sweetly, looking up at him. He's very tall and well muscled. So is most of the male staff. They're not technically security, but they might as well be. How are she and the guys *ever* going to make this work?

Bronx County Psychiatric is divided by wing. There are several lockdown wards, where the patients—prisoners, really—never leave their rooms, not even for meal time. Thankfully, John Doe—Mr.

Healy—is on the fourth floor, where the patients enjoy a degree of freedom.

The elevator door opens, and there he is in the common area, listlessly watching television. The man beside him is carrying on a whispered conversation with the characters on the screen, but Healy doesn't seem to notice. Nor does he particularly seem to be paying attention to the program. His mind is exactly where his life is—in limbo. He's obviously depressed, and no wonder.

She's almost flattened by an attack of conscience. How could she be conspiring with the people who let this wonderful man rot in his confused solitude for *weeks*? She takes Gecko and his friends at their word when they say that Healy's injury was an accident. But how could they wait until now before taking action to save him?

Why am I helping these guys? Is it just because I like Gecko? Am I that shallow?

Yet, all the evidence to the contrary, she's positive that, at his core, Gecko is a good person.

Surely I can't be wrong about something that important, that basic!

Besides, how can a spoiled rich girl judge kids like Gecko, Arjay, and Terence? They've known nothing but hardship, while she's known only private schools, private clubs, private yachts, and doors that are always open because of who her father is.

"Hi, John."

Healy looks up and beams at her. His smile seems all the brighter for how rarely it appears these days. "Hey, stranger. How's the orientation coming along?"

"Done. I'm chief psychiatrist now."

"Don't I wish!" he exclaims. "Then you could check me out of here."

"Well, maybe not all the way out," she says lightly. "But how about I drag you down to the cafeteria for a cup of coffee?"

He makes a face. "The inmates are only allowed decaf here. It tastes like raw sewage."

"Hot chocolate, then," she coaxes. "And I'll throw in my brilliant conversation."

He stands. "You're a lifesaver. I need to get off the planet Krypton for a while."

The cafeteria is on the main floor at the rear of the building. Its walls are painted a deep pink.

"Research shows that this is the most restful color," she says, plunking two steaming cups onto the table in front of them. "At least, that's what the head nurse said at orientation."

"It looks like someone blew up a flamingo farm," he comments cheerfully.

Roxanne notes the difference in Healy when he's removed from the atmosphere of the ward. His mood is lighter—he's almost relaxed. You can actually see his shoulders descending from up around his ears as his tension eases.

She's tense enough for the two of them. But she can't let Healy notice that. Everything has to seem normal. She sips at her drink and tries not to stare at the doorway leading into the kitchen. Behind that wall, she knows, lies another door, the one that leads to the alley—where Gecko and his friends will be waiting very soon now.

The sign on the small panel truck reads: AJAX LINEN SERVICE.

"It's a tight ride," Gecko confirms as he tools the vehicle on to the uptown FDR. All rides are tight when the opportunity to drive is as rare as a Fourth of July blizzard.

"I still say we should have jacked something with a little more style," Terence grumbles.

"We've got all the style we need," Arjay insists. "If anybody spots us behind the hospital, we look like we're making a delivery. Let's keep our heads in the game. This is for all the marbles."

"And for Mr. Healy," Gecko adds, his knuckles white on the wheel.

Terence grunts, but he can't deny the truth of it. Up until now, his life has been mostly about image—acting tough, looking cool, coming off gangster. But tonight he sees that image is worth squat. When you're playing for stakes this high, only results count. If they can't make this happen, nothing else matters.

They fly up the FDR and hit the Willis Avenue

Bridge doing seventy. The red brake lights come out of nowhere. Gecko stomps on the pedal and pumps the truck to a lurching stop.

Arjay is alarmed. "What's all this traffic?"

Gecko throws the gears into reverse in an attempt to back them out. Too late. A crush of vehicles has filled in the roadway behind them. They're locked into the snarl.

Crouched in the payload behind the front seat, Terence straightens up and peers over the stopped cars. Lights flash in the distance. "Accident up ahead. How long till we get through?"

"How should I know?" snaps Gecko.

"Calm down," soothes Arjay.

But there's nothing to be calm about. They have scripted every minute detail of this operation. Except one: what if they're late for their own breakout?

"Rox!" Gecko moans in agony. According to their timetable, at exactly 9:20 she's going to bring Healy to the kitchen exit. "If she opens that door and we're not there—"

"You're the hotshot driver," Terence exclaims. "Get us there!"

"We'll get there! We'll get there!" Arjay insists, trying to convince himself as much as the others.

"What if we can't?" Gecko demands, his voice rising.

Fifteen minutes go by. They have not moved a single inch.

"This better not be some little fender bender!" Terence seethes. "If we're going back to jail over this, I want somebody's spleen lying on the road!"

Three pairs of eyes switch from the unmoving jam to the dashboard clock: 8:40 . . . 8:50 . . . 9:00 . . .

"We're so dead," moans Gecko. "Poor Rox!"

"She'll be fine," says Terence bitterly. "We're the ones who'll be taking the fall."

"Maybe not," breathes Arjay. "Look!"

The traffic is suddenly moving again, as if nothing ever happened.

"Floor it!" orders Terence.

Gecko is already weaving the panel truck through the gaps that are opening between cars. They pass a wrecker with a stalled SUV on its hoist, and Terence awards it an obscene gesture.

"Spleenless fool!"

"Can we make it?" asks Arjay.

In answer, Gecko wheels down avenues and side streets, running stoplights, and using the sidewalk as a passing lane.

The dashboard clock reads 9:17 as they pull up to the access lane behind Bronx County Psychiatric Hospital. The guardhouse is empty, the entrance padlocked, just as Roxanne said.

Terence heads for the rear doors, cracking his knuckles as he goes. "One open gate, coming up."

And then a bent figure appears out of the shadows.

"Freeze!" hisses Arjay.

Barely daring to breathe, they watch as the man shuffles across the access way, shining a flashlight at the gate and the alley behind it.

"Rox didn't say anything about a night watchman," Gecko whispers.

The clock: 9:18.

Their heartbeats seem to reverberate inside the truck. The figure ambles to the corner and disappears around the front of the building.

"Now!" Arjay rasps.

Terence is out and on the gate in a flash, his hand just a blur as he works on the lock.

9:19.

The barrier swings wide.

The linen truck enters the lane. Terence shuts the gate and jumps back inside. The three pan the rear of the building, but see nothing other than barred windows and thick stone walls.

Sweating, Gecko halts at a row of Dumpsters, and there it is—a heavy steel door with no knob on the outside.

9:20. Zero hour.

CHAPTER TWENTY-NINE

The paper is titled "Introduction to Physics—Wave/Particle Duality." Due date—

"That's tomorrow!" exclaims Margaret Browning Fitzner.

August Fitzner looks up from his *Wall Street Journal*. "What's tomorrow?"

"This homework. Roxie needs it if she's going to school straight from Brittany's tomorrow."

She picks up the phone, checks a list, and speed-dials. "Hello, Brittany. It's Mrs. Fitzner. Can I speak to Roxanne for a minute, please? . . . She *isn't*? But—"

Her husband is out of his chair and pacing. "She's not there?"

"Sorry to bother you, Brittany. I must have the wrong friend." She hangs up and turns to her husband in alarm.

"Don't worry," he says grimly. "I have a pretty good idea where she is."

* * *

Deputy Chief Mike Delancey is still in the office. He normally works fairly late. But when the chief is out of town, he practically lives at One Police Plaza.

He's finally heading for the door when the call comes through from August Fitzner.

"Braxton," Delancey calls to the sergeant, "what did I do with the file on that Gecko kid—the one who's mixed up with Augie Fitzner's daughter?"

A few minutes later, he's back at his desk, rifling through the folder. Graham Fosse. Street name—Gecko. There's his mug shot. Delancey remembers their meeting in the school, scaring the kid off—obviously not well enough.

Reaching for yet another pear from the basket on the cabinet, he scans the description of the halfway house. The kid caught a real break to get picked for something like that. Stupid of him to risk it all for a girl, even a cute one like Roxie. Too bad.

His eyes fall on the picture of Douglas Healy, who runs the home situation for Social Services. He frowns. Why does this guy look so familiar? Do I know him?

He catches sight of the bulletin board just outside his office door. The John Doe Wall of Fame, they call it. At any given time, the city has between fifty and a hundred people, living and dead, that it can't identify.

He takes a bite of the pear, and, painfully, the side of his mouth. He barely notices the taste of blood.

For there, hidden in the middle of the John Doe Wall of Fame, is Douglas Healy.

He rushes over to read the details: *John Doe #1453Y. Turned up at Yorkville Medical Center in a comatose state; acute retrograde amnesia; no measurable improvement; transferred 10/23 to Bronx County Psychiatric Hospital.*

Delancey is thunderstruck. Three days ago, he was instrumental in getting Roxanne Fitzner assigned there as a volunteer.

Oh, Roxie, what have you gotten yourself into?

He reaches for the phone.

The cafeteria is open around the clock for twenty-four-hour shift workers. Besides Healy and Roxanne, the only other customer is a tired-looking nurse having a late sandwich in the far corner.

As 9:20 approaches, Roxanne's stomach churns like the rapids of the Colorado River.

Even Healy notices. "Are you feeling okay?"

"I'm fine," she says faintly, taking a sip of her very cold hot chocolate. Her system is so upset that it's all she can do to keep it down.

"You push yourself too hard," Healy chides her. "Between that high-powered private school and so many hours volunteering—at Yorkville they used to joke about setting up a cot for you behind the nurses' station."

She glances at her watch. Not quite yet. They

can't be seen standing around the kitchen. The timing has to be perfect.

"I mean, it's great that you care so much," Healy continues, "but if you let yourself get so run down . . ."

Come on, come on, come on! she exhorts the second hand as it creeps lazily around the dial.

". . . then the next group of volunteers will have to visit *you*—are you even listening to me?"

She leaps to her feet so suddenly that her chair overturns with a clatter. "Let's go!"

"Go? Where?"

She grabs his wrist and hauls him across the cafeteria to the kitchen.

"What's going on?" he demands.

She regards him helplessly. "You'll have to trust me."

"Trust you for *what*?"

She leads him into the kitchen, moving past dishwashers and cooks, who look up in surprise. The exit is dead ahead, at the end of a line of stainless steel refrigerators. Roxanne heads for it, dragging along a bewildered Healy. The second hand of her watch is coming around again.

9:20 on the nose.

It's now obvious to Healy that she's taking him outside. "This is crazy!"

"Whatever happens," she quavers, "always remember that I'm your friend." She hip-checks the security bar, and the heavy door swings wide. Arjay stands there, his hulking frame filling the opening.

"How's it going, Mr. Healy?"

With a gasp of shock, Healy pulls back, poised for flight. But Arjay is ready. He reaches out and grabs the group leader's arm before he can escape. In an instant, Terence is there, and Healy is immobilized.

A loud buzzer sounds within the building. Roxanne and the boys are startled. The kitchen staff is staring at them, but how could they have sounded the alarm so soon?

"Let's go!" hisses Arjay.

They hustle Healy out into the lane and stuff him in the back of the truck. Roxanne jumps up after him, with Arjay and Terence bringing up the rear.

Behind the wheel, Gecko looks over his shoulder. "Is that an alarm I hear?"

Healy stares at him. "Gecko?"

Arjay slams the double doors shut. "Go! Go!"

Gecko throws the truck into reverse and begins retreating up the alley. In the side mirror he sees the night watchman hustle to the gate and begin fiddling with the padlock.

Gecko leans on the horn and speeds up, but the watchman is determined to get the padlock back in place.

Swallowing hard, Gecko presses down on the accelerator. "Come on, mister, don't be a hero!"

Frantically, the man snaps the lock shut and dives clear. A split second later, the truck blasts backward out of the alley, tearing the gate clean off its moorings, and tossing it in a shower of sparks into the middle of the street.

Gecko throws the gearshift into drive and burns rubber. A new sound reaches their ears, mingling with the Klaxon from Bronx County Psychiatric—police sirens.

Three squad cars scream around the corner. The lead cruiser drives up onto the broken gate, razor wire slashing into the front tires. It spins out and stalls, front end deflated. The second swerves to avoid it and jumps the curb. The undercarriage comes down on a concrete flower box, and the vehicle is hung up there, front wheels spinning.

The third car howls past, barreling after the linen truck.

"Gecko, why aren't you stopping?" Roxanne shrills. "That's a policeman back there!"

"Hang on," Gecko orders grimly. He wrenches the wheel, and the truck jounces across the sidewalk, plows over the muddy leaves of a vacant lot, and shudders onto the pavement of the next street over. The cop hesitates, then goes the long way around, screeching through two right turns.

For a moment, Gecko thinks he's in the clear. Then the cruiser reappears in the mirror, far back, but gaining. Gecko presses the pedal as far as it will go, coaxing a little more speed, but not much. A panel truck is not built for racing. The cruiser grows larger in the mirror. The wail of the siren swirls all around them, filling the van.

"Lose him!" Terence pleads.

Gecko looks around wildly. He doesn't know the Bronx. How is he supposed to elude a cop on his home turf, driving a faster vehicle?

The truck bounces over a rise, and he sees it. Just ahead, the road follows a small bridge over a shadowed gully. If he can get down into the hollow before his pursuer reaches the rise, he just might be able to disappear, tricking the cop into "following" him across the bridge.

He steers for the span, but at the last second he cuts the lights and threads the needle between the barrier at the side of the road and the bridge rail.

In the back, Arjay, Terence, Roxanne, and Healy are tossed around like Ping-Pong balls as the truck lurches down the embankment. Wildly, Gecko pumps at the brake in an attempt to slow their descent. Nothing helps. He has made this move with no idea of where they're going, or how they can ever get out.

Desperately, he squints into the gloom, grappling for the tiniest bit of night sight. Suddenly, out of nowhere, a concentrated beam of light shines directly in front of him, illuminating the bottom of the gully, lined with a double row of shiny tracks.

The realization almost knocks him off his seat. *This isn't a ditch! It's a railway line! And that light is—*

CHAPTER THIRTY

Fueled by pure panic, Gecko yanks on the wheel just as the locomotive explodes out of the darkness. The steering mechanism screeches its protest as they skid toward a collision with the speeding train. At the last second, the tires bite into the earth, and the truck makes the sharp turn, moving along beside the rattling freight cars, avoiding disaster by no more than a few inches.

Arjay peels himself off the wall of the payload and peers over Gecko's shoulder. "What was that? Where are we?"

"We're driving beside a train," Gecko says faintly. "I'm pretty sure we lost that cop."

"And *I'm* pretty sure I need to change my underwear!" seethes Terence. "You trying to kill us, dog?"

Roxanne's voice is barely a whisper. "What do we do now?"

Gecko has absolutely no idea. He's not even

certain the truck has enough guts to get them back up the embankment to the street.

They parallel the train for a few minutes until it passes. Then they continue on slowly, looking for a spot that's a little less steep.

The ascent is slow and messy. The spinning tires kick up so much mud that Gecko has to run the windshield wipers just to see. At long last, the white van that descended into the hollow emerges a filthy brown one.

Gecko leans out the window. The Ajax Linen Service logo is completely obliterated by grime. "The cops'll never recognize us now."

"Not unless we get pulled over for Driving While Disgusting," Terence agrees.

"Even so, stay off the main roads," Arjay advises. "By now, the whole police force must know about us."

Healy speaks up. "Would somebody mind telling me what's going on?"

As they start off, moving cautiously south toward Manhattan, Arjay begins the long story.

"Your name is Douglas Healy, and you're the founder of an alternative halfway house. . . ."

Gecko concentrates on the road and their surroundings, but keeps an ear open for any sign that the group leader's memory is coming back.

The initial indicators are all bad. "I don't recognize you," he tells them. "I remember Gecko from

Yorkville, but the rest is a blank. I've never even heard of Douglas Healy, and that's *me*!"

"Keep an open mind," Roxanne pleads. "Sooner or later something has to ring a bell."

On the slow serpentine trip, Gecko sees a number of police cars and makes a point of veering down side streets to avoid a close encounter. Their vehicle may look different covered in mud, but it's still a panel truck. Surely by now, Bronx County Psychiatric has taken a head count and realized that they're short one John Doe.

Behind him, Arjay is feeding Healy his own life story from the personal file on his computer. Gecko recites along mentally as he drives—Healy's childhood in New York; his arrest for assault at the age of fifteen—a fight that broke out while he was selling fireworks across state lines with an older cousin: thirty-two months in juvie, followed by a comeback in which he put himself through college and returned to Manhattan to work as an accountant. Next, the death of his parents just a few months apart, leaving him with no living relatives. And most important of all, his decision to pool his modest inheritance with a Garfield grant to found a program to help juvenile offenders get their lives back on track—just as young Douglas Healy had.

The group leader listens with a look on his face like he's watching a movie of the week—it's an interesting story, but that's all. No recognition.

"I want to believe you—I *do* believe you. But I don't remember it. Not one word."

"Come on, Mr. Healy," urges Terence. "*Please* think harder!"

The truck rattles over the bridge to Manhattan, and Gecko heads downtown along Second Avenue. "Where should we let you off?" he calls over his shoulder to Roxanne.

"I'm staying with you."

"No way," Arjay tells her. "Who knows what they'll stick on our rap sheet after tonight."

"I'm not leaving until this gets settled one way or the other," she says stoutly. "I want to see what happens to you—*all* of you."

"We can't let you get mixed up in this!" Gecko interjects.

"You want to throw her out of a moving truck?" asks Terence. "Let her be."

Second Avenue is slow and plodding, but not for Gecko, who weaves in and out, slipping through improbably narrow spaces. Buildings and storefronts gradually become familiar as they approach their own neighborhood. They've done it—Healy is out; their escape is complete. Another brilliant getaway for Gecko Fosse. But this time there's little to celebrate.

With a skillful tap on the accelerator, he twists the linen truck out of the traffic flow and backs into a line of parked vehicles. "We're here."

Arjay peers out the front. The sign reads AJAX

LINEN SERVICE. "This is where we boosted the truck!"

Gecko shifts into park and separates the "hot" wires. The engine dies.

The five of them—Gecko, Arjay, Terence, Roxanne, and Healy—climb out and bustle down the avenue. The group leader has no coat, and hugs himself against the biting wind.

Gecko sneaks a glance at him, searching for even the slightest sign of recognition in his any-color eyes. No, Healy is rubbernecking like a tourist—even when they turn down Ninety-seventh Street toward their building.

"Hey, Mr. Healy," Terence ventures, "this is where we chucked that rye bread and pegged Ms. Vaughn."

Healy's dismay multiplies when Gecko ushers him up the cement steps. "This is—home?"

Arjay tries to insert his key, and the front door swings wide. "Open sesame," he says sarcastically. "Lock's busted for a change. Lucky we've got nothing worth stealing."

They start up the dingy stairs.

"Yeah, people really *do* live like this," Terence informs Roxanne. "It's not just on *America's Most Wanted*."

"I've been in walk-ups before," she defends herself.

"We're busy, man," Arjay hisses to Terence. "Lose the sociology lecture."

The truth is they've run out of planning. Not one of them honestly expected to make it this far. Now what? When do they give up on Healy's memory and ask him to flat-out lie for them?

Arjay opens the door, ushering the others in ahead of him. Gecko reaches for the light switch.

And then all hell breaks loose.

CHAPTER THIRTY-ONE

Something hard swings past Gecko's face. He hears the crash of impact, breaking glass, but the cry of pain comes from Arjay. Before Gecko can react, he is shoved from behind. His face collides with the wall, and he tastes blood.

The scream that follows is unmistakable. Roxanne.

"Rox!" He tries to leap at the unseen attacker, but a punch slams into his stomach, doubling him over.

The lights flash on to reveal a terrifying scene in the apartment. Two intruders restrain the struggling Arjay, who is bleeding badly from his cheek. Another grapples with Healy in the galley kitchen. Still another stands threateningly over Gecko, while keeping an eye on Roxanne, who is sprawled on the living room floor.

Gecko is about to make another run at his opponent when he catches sight of the fifth and final intruder. DeAndre has Terence in a headlock, the blade of a large knife pressed against his captive's throat.

"I'll cut him, yo."

Considering the wildness of the moment, his voice is dull and flat. Not a threat, but a statement of fact. Terence doesn't speak, but his eyes are full of horror.

DeAndre pans the apartment, taking in Healy and Roxanne. "Who's this, your grandpa? And your sister. Real Hallmark."

"What do you want?" Arjay sputters.

DeAndre shuffles forward with Terence, never relaxing the deadly position of the knife. "We're taking the yo for a little heart-to-heart. It's got nothing to do with you, so just mind your own business while we walk out of here."

Healy, the only adult present, can keep silent no longer. "Now, wait one minute!"

"Step off, old man!" DeAndre thunders. "I got no beef with you—yet. On the couch—everybody! It's all over soon, so long as nobody does anything stupid."

Arjay hesitates, but with the blade at Terence's jugular, they have little choice. The big boy allows his captors to hustle him into the living room. Warily, Healy and Gecko follow. Terence shoots them a look of frenzied pleading.

Terence, you idiot! Gecko wails inwardly. *Why'd you have to do this to yourself? To all of us!*

He has never been a Florian fan—their partnership has always been a forced affair, fed by necessity, not any kind of friendship. Yet Terence's own words resonate in an endless loop in his brain: *You watch out for your dogs . . .*

"Nice and easy," DeAndre approves. "Relax, watch a little TV. Don't mind us, we're just leaving." He continues to shove Terence in the direction of the door.

Gecko reaches for the TV remote, sitting on the set next to Healy's old bowling award. The decision is made in a fraction of a second, the reaction time of any good getaway driver. Gecko snatches up the trophy, watching in satisfaction as the bowler breaks off yet again. Before anyone has a chance to see the exposed metal spike, the missile is airborne, flung with all his strength at the razor-cut boy.

The point buries itself in DeAndre's forearm. A howled curse, and the knife clatters to the floor.

It's the break Terence has been waiting for, and he doesn't squander it. Just a blur, he's gone—not toward the door, which is blocked by DeAndre's henchmen, but into the large bedroom. In a flash, the window is open, and he's scrambling onto the fire escape.

For a heartbeat the world stands still, as combatants on both sides process this latest development. Then there's a mad stampede after Terence. DeAndre stoops to pick up his fallen knife. Healy lunges for it, sending it spinning out of reach with a desperate kick. His legs slide out from under him, and he goes down beside the wreckage of the trophy. DOUGLAS HEALY—2ND PLACE. This thing is *his*?

Arjay throws off his captors as easily as he might shrug out of a jacket and joins the race for the window. DeAndre gets there first, with Gecko hot on his heels. Arjay fights one against four to clamber onto the wrought-iron landing. Healy picks himself off the floor and brings up the rear.

Roxanne grabs his arm. "You're not ready for this! You just got out of the hospital!"

Healy shoots her a helpless look and climbs over the sill. His sneakers come down on the slats of the fire escape, creating a deep percussive gonging.

He pulls up short. *I've heard that sound before!*

He takes in his surroundings, pop-eyed with discovery.

I've been in this place before!

Once the dam has been breached, nothing can hold back the flood of memory. It's a deluge.

Roxanne stares in horror from the bedroom. Healy's expression might be that of someone whose head is being crushed inside a vise. The danger forgotten, she's out the window and at his side. "Are you hurt?"

"No, I'm—" He teeters on the landing, unsure of the very gravity that connects him to the planet. "I think I'm—who broke my bowling trophy?"

He's interrupted by a cry from below as DeAndre vaults over the railing and drops onto the fleeing

Terence. The two crash to the stairs, fists already flying in full-on combat. A moment later, Gecko is in the middle of it, pounding and being pounded. Arjay's tree-trunk arms wade into the fray. It's a full-fledged brawl, a brutal wrestling match perched thirty feet off the ground.

Punches rain on Gecko like hammer blows. They're outnumbered five to three against tougher, street-hardened competition. DeAndre has Terence against the steps, forcing him under the rail to a devastating drop.

"Hey! No!" Terence cries in terror, his torso twisting in midair, his arms flailing for something to hold on to.

"Hang on!" Arjay gets a massive hand around Terence's ankle and pulls back with his considerable brawn.

"Oof!"

A knee connects with Arjay's groin, and he's writhing in agony. Two pairs of arms take control of Gecko from behind. As quickly as that, the battle is lost. Healy's trio is at the mercy of the crew from New York.

The razor-cut boy's voice is liquid nitrogen. "Throw them off."

Sudden blinding light turns the night into day as the drama on the fire escape is caught in the nexus of two powerful flashlight beams.

"NYPD—*freeze*!"

Deputy Chief Delancey and his driver, a uniformed patrolman, peer up at them from street level.

DeAndre's assessment of the situation is quick and decisive. "Only two cops!" Releasing Terence, he vaults to the next landing, the rest of the crew hot on his heels. The five leap from the second floor, kicking over trash cans to create a buffer between themselves and capture. One twists his ankle and sprawls on the pavement. The others hurdle the debris and sprint for freedom.

They have just pounded onto the sidewalk when two squad cars screech to a stop directly in front of them. Their only move is to jump backward to keep from being run down. Four officers appear, guns drawn. It's the work of only a few seconds before DeAndre and company are up against the wall in handcuffs.

Delancey trains his flashlight on the figures on the fire escape. "All right, the rest of you come down. And keep your hands where I can see them."

Roxanne peers over the rail. "Uncle Mike—it's me!"

The deputy chief lets out a sharp exhalation of relief. "Roxie—thank God! Did anybody hurt you?"

"I'm fine!" she calls back. "These are the good guys!"

Delancey is not convinced. "According to the staff at Bronx County Psychiatric, not even *you're* the good guys. Where's Douglas Healy?"

Healy stands up. "Right here. These boys are in my charge. I remember everything now."

"Sounds pretty convenient. Who was in charge of them while you were John Doe?"

The uncomfortable silence is punctuated by slamming of car doors as DeAndre and his crew are locked in the cruisers.

"It isn't as bad as it sounds," Roxanne ventures finally.

The deputy chief shakes his head grimly. "Let me be the judge of that."

CHAPTER THIRTY-TWO

After the counting of heads and checking of IDs, at last Delancey is satisfied that everyone is who they claim to be. He releases the cruisers with their collars, and instructs his driver to wait in the car.

The officer is dubious. "You sure about that, chief?"

"Not really," he admits. "But I can't resist a good story, and I have a feeling I'm about to hear an epic."

Upstairs in the apartment, the celebration over the return of Healy's memory is tempered by the fact that they've been caught. And that can mean only one thing.

"I don't care," Gecko says bravely. "Everything that happened was our fault, and now you're okay. Going back to jail is a small price to pay."

"We're so sorry," Arjay adds. "Can you ever forgive us?"

The group leader looks unhappy. "God, you

guys—I know what it's like to be in your spot. Everything I did was because I was there once myself. But I don't know if I can help you out of this one."

Terence can barely lift his gaze off the floor. "It's all on me, Mr. Healy. These guys—they tried to do the right thing. I'm the one who kept screwing up. It's like I can't handle the fact that somebody's trying to give me a break."

"Then you're in luck," Arjay tells him bitterly. "I don't think any more breaks will be coming our way from here on in."

"I'll talk to Uncle Mike," Roxanne promises. "I can make him understand."

"He seemed real understanding when he was warning me to stay away from you," Gecko reminds her. "And I'm sure he's thrilled that I did such a great job of it."

On that note, the door swings open, and Deputy Chief Delancey is upon them, glaring as only an angry policeman can. And they are indeed quite a sight—battle-scarred, bruised, and bloody from the struggle on the fire escape. Even Healy and Roxanne, though unmarked, are wild-eyed and disheveled from their frenetic escape and the altercation with DeAndre and his crew.

"All right," the deputy chief growls. "Start talking. And remember, I've been a cop for thirty-five years. The CIA wishes they had a BS-meter as good as mine."

Healy speaks up. "None of us are angels here, but they're not bad kids. I'd stake my reputation on it."

"That's one vote of confidence from the escaped mental patient. Now, how about a little explanation?"

"What would you have done in their place?" the group leader persists. "I was the only thing standing between these boys and hell, and when I got hurt—"

"Interesting topic," approves the deputy chief. "Your injury. How did it happen?"

"It was my bad—" Terence begins.

Arjay cuts him off. "We're all in the same boat. Whatever we did, we'll take the blame together." He looks at Gecko, who nods.

"I think there's plenty of blame to go around," Delancey offers, losing patience.

Arjay shrugs. "We just wanted to look around a little. We were out of jail, but our lives were programmed twenty-five hours a day. So we tried to sneak out. Mr. Healy came after us and he fell."

The deputy chief's eyes shoot sparks. "And nobody helped him over the rail?"

"It really was an accident," Healy assures him. The fine points of the actual event are still vague in his mind as his returning memory fills in the details. But he believes it with all his heart.

Delancey grunts noncommittally. "Go on."

His rumbling voice grave, Arjay recounts the trio's decision to carry on their halfway-house routine while praying for Healy's recovery.

The veteran cop is skeptical. "I wasn't born yesterday, kid. Social Services—they've got checks and balances for this kind of thing. Reports not filed, absences from school, no-shows in therapy and community service."

"But we did all that," Gecko insists. "We filed the reports by computer and kept going to group and the B.I.D. And at school, we made sure we had perfect attendance and good grades."

Delancey regards them in amazement. "Are you telling me that you were scot-free—for all these weeks, you could have bought a bus ticket and disappeared off the face of the earth! And you chose to stay here and stick with a group leader who couldn't have told you from Adam, doing everything you were supposed to, including *homework*?"

Terence indicates Arjay. "Trust me, the teacher isn't born who's more of a hard-ass than the big dog."

"In the meantime," Gecko takes up the tale, "I visited the hospital to keep an eye on Mr. Healy, and that's where I met Rox."

"The doctors kept saying the amnesia would go away, Uncle Mike," Roxanne pleads. "You can't blame the guys for waiting till they had their group leader back. Otherwise, the halfway house would have been closed up."

"Who could have predicted that they'd take someone who isn't nuts and stick him in a nuthouse?" Arjay continues.

"*I* could have predicted it," Delancey offers. "I've worked for the city for thirty-five years. The genius of bureaucracy can't amaze me anymore."

"Well, we couldn't let that happen to him," Gecko concludes. "So we broke him out, and you caught us. End of story."

"Except for the five gang members we arrested on your fire escape," the deputy chief reminds them.

"They go to our school," Arjay explains. "We've been trying to stay away from them, but they're pretty persistent."

Delancey nods. "They were no strangers to the cops who collared them. Good people to stay away from."

Healy turns to the deputy chief. "I'm back. I'm fine. It's not like you'd be turning them loose. With me, they're still in the custody of the Department of Juvenile Corrections. Everything they did—even when it was wrong—they did it for all the right reasons. And surely they get some brownie points for sticking with the program even when there was no one around to make them do it."

"You're asking me to make an awful lot go away," Delancey grunts.

"It's for me too," Roxanne reminds him. "*And* my family."

He frowns. "Is there a stolen laundry truck I need to know about?"

"No, sir," Gecko says stoutly. "We put it back exactly where we found it."

There's a long pause. The cop lets out a heavy sigh. "All right. But there's one thing you have to do for me, and this one's not negotiable."

"Anything," Healy promises.

"You two—" Delancey indicates Gecko and Roxanne. "You're through. You're not sweethearts, you're not friends; I don't even want you on the same buddy list on MySpace."

"But, Uncle Mike—" she protests.

"No buts, Roxie. Think about Gecko. He doesn't have the kind of safety net you do. If he screws up, it's all the way."

Gecko and Roxanne exchange a sad look. Gecko knows the break he's being offered is nothing short of colossal, but right now the price seems very high.

Terence awards him a slap in the back of the head. "What are you even thinking about, dog? Take the deal. No offense," he adds to Roxanne. "If I ever need an undercover agent at the freaky farm, you're number one on my list."

"Shut up, Terence," Arjay orders firmly.

"Well?" Delancey prompts. "Do I have your word?"

Gecko takes in Roxanne's crestfallen expression. She isn't happy, but she's smart enough to recognize that they really have no choice.

"We'll do it," he promises unhappily.

"And this time make it stick. Or else." The deputy chief stands up. "I hope the fact that none of you are crawling on the floor kissing my feet doesn't mean you don't appreciate this second chance. God, more like fifteenth chance." He turns to Roxanne. "Need a ride home?"

It isn't an offer.

Gecko watches them go. Roxanne holds his gaze through the very last sliver of doorway.

Get a grip, Rox.

CHAPTER THIRTY-THREE

Ms. Debra Vaughn rings the buzzer of the apartment on Ninety-seventh Street at exactly nine a.m. on Wednesday morning.

Upstairs, she is greeted by group leader Douglas Healy and his three charges. Graham Fosse, Arjay Moran, and Terence Florian are neatly dressed and on their best behavior, but nothing can hide the cuts and bruises on their faces.

"Lacrosse tryouts," Healy explains. "They take it very seriously at that school."

"You should see the other guys," adds Terence.

The look he gets from Arjay would take the paint off the front door.

"No sports," Ms. Vaughn orders. "No extracurricular activities of any sort. Maintaining their grades is their only priority."

The group leader brightens. "Well, there we've got some really good news—"

"I've seen the reports," the social worker interrupts coldly. "Let's move on to the visual inspection of the apartment."

All the attention Ms. Vaughn has never been able to give them because of her heavy caseload is now focused on these eight hundred square feet of living space. Every finger mark and dust bunny is brought under her microscope. She has no way of knowing that the four of them have spent the last twenty-four hours cleaning the place and restocking the refrigerator with healthy food. And still she's able to find several examples of "unspeakable filth."

Healy tries to make light of it. "I guess we're not going to make the front cover of *Good Housekeeping*."

"This may seem like a joke to you, Mr. Healy, but dust and dirt are more than just a hygiene problem. Slovenly habits spill over into poor discipline. Remember—a failure in discipline is what put them into the juvenile corrections system to begin with. And a failure in discipline is what's likely to send them back."

Gecko, Arjay, and Terence exchange looks of dismay. They have gotten away with putting their group leader in the hospital, weeks unsupervised, countless deceptions, and engineering a breakout from a mental institution. After surviving all that, surely they can't be shipped off to juvie because there are too many crumbs in the toaster.

All at once, Ms. Vaughn draws in a horrified

breath. "What is that weapon doing in this house?"

"What?" Healy is close to the edge. "There's no weapon here!"

Blazing with indignation, she marches straight to the TV. Atop it sit the two pieces of the broken bowling trophy.

Overcome with relief, the group leader laughs out loud. "That's just my old bowling prize. It got knocked over a few weeks ago, and no matter what kind of glue I use, it just keeps falling apart on me."

"Article two, subsection four of the Uniform Code of Alternative Living Arrangements for Youth Offenders clearly bans all sharp objects."

Healy is astonished. "It's a bowling trophy, not a samurai sword!"

"A glass bottle is not a weapon either," the social worker lectures. "But when you break it, producing a jagged edge, it becomes a *lethal* one. This exposed spike is a material breach of the code—which means that this place can be shut down on the spot, and the boys returned to juvenile detention for completion of sentence—"

"What kind of person are you?" Healy explodes. "You've been gunning for us since day one! It wouldn't satisfy you if these boys solve global warming! You want them behind bars, and that's where you're determined to put them! Well, I'm going to fight you every step of the way!"

"Let me finish," Ms. Vaughn continues. "By law,

you *could* be shut down. But in view of all the remarkable progress you've made with these boys, I'm not going to do that."

Gecko's head snaps up. "You're not?"

"Frankly," the social worker tells them, "if I didn't see it with my own eyes, I never would have believed that anyone could turn these three into decent productive teenagers. Vigilance and supervision—that's the key. You never took your eyes off them for a second. Congratulations, Mr. Healy. I underestimated you."

His temper tantrum barely cooled, the group leader can only stare at her, speechless.

"However," she goes on, "this trophy should be a warning to you. I've been a social worker for twenty years, and absolutely *nothing* gets by me. I can take a look around this apartment and know everything that's been going on in your lives. You have no secrets from me. . . ."

As she rambles on about herself being all-knowing and all-seeing, Gecko, Arjay, and Terence struggle mightily not to snicker. Ms. Vaughn may be able to detect dust bunnies the size of microdots, but she doesn't have a clue that the man running her halfway house has spent several weeks hospitalized with amnesia, leaving his charges to fend for themselves. They can only imagine what articles and subsections of the Uniform Code of Alternative Living Arrangements for Youth Offenders they've been violating minute by minute.

Yet they keep their thoughts to themselves. Even Terence manages to fight down the impulse to mouth off. They stay focused on the big picture. Survival against all odds. Very sweet.

They thank the social worker and escort her not only to the door, but down the stairs and right into a taxi, just to make sure she's really gone. At that, she refuses to let the cabbie drive away until she sees the bowling trophy in the garbage. A stickler right to the very end.

Healy lets out a long breath. "Well, guys, we did it. *You* did it, really. Because it never could have happened if you hadn't kept up with school, and community service, and therapy."

"Freaky," Terence agrees. "Doing the right thing turns out to be the right thing. I must be bugging."

As they head back upstairs, they find Mrs. Liebowitz waiting for them on the fourth-floor landing.

"It's good to see you, Mr. Healy. I guess my suspicions that something might have happened to you were unfounded."

Healy beams at her. "I'm fine, Mrs. Liebowitz." Having passed the Ms. Vaughn test, he isn't overly concerned with the building snoop. "In fact, I've never felt better."

As soon as he says it, he realizes that it's true. The flood of returning recollection out on the fire escape was violent to the point of pain, like having his brain pumped full of helium. But since then, his recovery has been peaceful and complete. He's no longer consciously aware of memories coming back to him. Now he simply reaches for them and they're there. It seems like the ultimate luxury after so many weeks when he would try to look back and find only empty space.

The one thing that haunts him is what might have happened if the fight with DeAndre's crew hadn't returned him to the fire escape. Would he still be in that awful fog? Yes, Gecko, Arjay, and Terence caused his original accident. But they never gave up on him when a thousand other kids in their place would have taken off. If he didn't know it before, he knows it now: he picked exactly the right three boys.

"I almost forgot." Mrs. Liebowitz hands Arjay a large manila envelope. "This came for you today. It wouldn't fit in your mail slot, and I didn't think you'd want to be disturbed when you were entertaining such an important visitor." She frowns. "It looks like a management contract for a professional musician, but how could that be? How would someone in a halfway house have the freedom to join a rock group?"

Healy snatches the package from Arjay and herds the boys inside Apartment 4B. "Thanks, Mrs. Liebowitz. I'll take care of it."

She watches the door close after them. "The letter says you're very good. . . ."

CHAPTER THIRTY-FOUR

Gecko Fosse is once more behind the wheel of an Infiniti M45—a red one this time. No, black. With a spoiler on the back. And a jet engine strapped onto the roof. He's even taken up his old hobby again—not thinking. He's still great at it. He's barely aware of the fact that he's actually not in any car, but sitting in group therapy, and that he isn't likely to find himself behind the wheel of a motor vehicle for a good long time.

But of course, Gecko's number one topic for not thinking is *her*. And not thinking about her only makes him think about her more.

Get over it! he berates himself. Do you have any idea how lucky you are? Healy's okay; you're not going back to Atchison. One girlfriend is a small price to pay for all that!

This is no ordinary therapy session—it's the final one. Dr. Avery has decided that the group has come as far as she can take them, and it's time to move on. They're having a farewell pizza party. Gecko isn't hungry.

Dr. Avery, who's still a knockout even while scrubbing tomato sauce off her chin, is emotional about this milestone. "I'm so proud of all of you. You've made such remarkable progress."

Terence is unimpressed. "You're the only one who's graduating, Doc. Social Services says we still have to do therapy. And now we've got to break in a whole new shrink."

Drew Roddenbury nods sadly. "The record companies won't cut me loose either. I'm still a threat to download another song."

"I'm a little worried about *you*, Gecko," Dr. Avery admits with a frown. "You've been gloomy and withdrawn for weeks."

I'm not having this conversation, Gecko tells himself firmly. Not on the last day of group. "It's just—you know—winter blahs."

The therapist smiles understandingly. "Winter blahs isn't a real diagnosis. You should be happy. The six months are almost over. Mr. Healy tells me your mom will be visiting in a couple of weeks."

Gecko nods without much enthusiasm. He's pleasantly surprised that she's able to juggle her three jobs and make the trip. But he has mixed feelings about it. Healy bent the rules and let him talk with her when she called to confirm that she'd be coming. Four and a half of the five minutes he was on the phone with her were spent lamenting Reuben's terrible fate in prison.

I know Reuben's got it rough, Mom, but can't something be just about me?

Arjay has enough enthusiasm for all three of them. "March eighteenth," he confirms brightly. "My folks are making a weekend of it, staying in a hotel."

He's excited almost to the point of giddiness. It's pretty comical, but no amount of relentless teasing from Terence can spoil Arjay's mood. To him, this visit is the light at the end of the tunnel, the first baby step of his return to the human race.

"My parents are giving it a pass," Terence puts in blandly. "My old man can't get away. He's got a lot of responsibility spreading misery and hearing-loss around the citizens of Southside Chicago. It'd be like Santa Claus trying to take Christmas Eve off."

Dr. Avery regards him in sympathy. "It's all fine as long as you're fine with it."

"Better than fine. Family lets you down, man. Big picture—find some dogs who've got your back."

"That's the kind of thinking that nearly got us killed," Arjay points out.

"The thinking wasn't the problem," Terence insists. "I just had the wrong dogs, that's all. Right now, I got all the crew I need—and that includes Healy."

For once, there's perfect agreement among the

trio. All three have made mistakes and suffered misfortunes. But the best thing that's happened to any of them is Douglas Healy.

Afterward, they're riding the elevator down to the lobby when Casey Wagner sidles up to Arjay. "The word downtown is This Page scored a recording deal."

Arjay nods. "I heard that too."

She probes further. "You should be celebrating."

"Not me. I quit four months ago. You were right. A guy in my situation can't be in a band."

She nods wanly, and the blue spikes of her hair tickle the bottom of his chin. "The best ones always burn out, or OD, or end up in trouble with the law. *No future*—that's what Johnny Rotten said." She takes a folded piece of paper and jams it into his palm.

"What's this?"

"My phone number. Use it." The elevator door opens, and she rushes off.

Arjay holds her note over the trash basket, then thinks better of it and stuffs it in his pocket. "No future" was once a perfect descriptor for him. Not anymore.

Healy collects them in the lobby and hands Terence a piece of paper. "This notice came from your school today. It says you have eleven overdue library books."

Terence crumples it up and tosses it in the garbage. "Yeah, I'm real scared. That librarian is a joke. She just stands there and lets people jack her stuff!"

Arjay rescues the form and smoothes it open. "That's why they call it a *lending* library," he explains patiently. "You're supposed to return what you borrow."

"Or what?" Terence scoffs. "Or nothing, man. If I ran a business like that, I'd be broke in a week."

Healy takes the notice back from Arjay. "I'm just impressed that you're reading."

"I'm a bookworm, all right," Terence agrees. "Hard-core. Ask me anything. Mockingbirds, the works."

"What's the food for, Mr. Healy?" Gecko puts in, indicating the plastic deli bag the group leader is carrying.

Healy passes out sandwiches. "Corned beef on rye from Shapiro's—best in the city. Dinner is on the run tonight. We've got an appointment. The new community service came through."

"Garbage picking, round two?" Terence queries. "That'll be fun when it's twenty below."

"We caught a break," the group leader assures them. "All indoor work. There's an old building at Bleecker and Bowery that the city's turning into a homeless shelter. How's your wrist action, Terence? You three are signed up as painters."

There's some good-natured grumbling. Between school and therapy, they've been on the go for twelve hours now.

Healy refuses to knuckle under to the complaining.

"Boo-hoo. Like you've never been tired before. Besides, it could be fun. They've got something like four hundred kids working on this project—community service, AmeriCorps, church and school groups, you name it."

The crabbing increases a subway ride later when they reach their destination. The building is a total wreck—crumbling plaster, broken stairs, dry rot, and dust, dust, dust.

"Are you sure four hundred of us are going to be enough?" Arjay wonders.

"It'll take at least that many to keep the ceiling from falling on our heads," Gecko adds sourly.

"I got a medical issue," puts in Terence. "Allergies, man."

"I know," Healy sympathizes. "You're allergic to work. Come on—I want you all to do this. It'll be good for you."

The complaining stops, even from Terence. Healy wants this, and he has the right to expect it after what he's done for them, and everything he's been through. Fair enough.

The group leader is right about the size of the crew. The meeting room is packed belly to belly with people, mostly teenagers. It's a chaotic scene—so many people clumsily stepping into painter's coveralls at the same moment, tripping over one another. Each worker is issued a piece of sandpaper and an air-filter mask.

Arjay frowns. "What's the mask for?"

That becomes apparent five minutes after they begin sanding the peeling walls. A dense cloud of dust hangs in the air like a fog, stinging their eyes and coating everything like a layer of volcanic ash.

"Man, there's always a cop around when it comes to busting people," Terence chokes. "But when four hundred kids are getting black lung disease, it's like, 'Health code? What health code?'"

"At least we're here because we've got no choice," Gecko mutters, barely able to make out the scrubbing action of his hand on the wall two feet in front of him. "What kind of an idiot actually *volunteers* for this torture?"

"A word of advice," comes a voice from behind. "Get a grip."

He wheels abruptly enough to pop the tendons in his neck. At first she's just a silhouette in the swirling haze of airborne powder, but he'd know that voice anywhere. Who volunteers for torture? Somebody who volunteers for everything. There's only one Roxanne—one in a million.

The rubber band holding his mask in place snaps on the right side. It's from the sheer size of his smile.

A millionaire, a deputy police chief, and the entire department of juvenile corrections may be able to control your life. But none of them can prevent a lightning strike.